DISCARD

THE TALISMAN

THE TALISMAN

Jonathan Aycliffe

Severn House
CPL

This title first published in Great Britain 2001 by
SEVERN HOUSE PUBLISHERS LTD of
9–15 High Street, Sutton, Surrey SM1 1DF.
This title first published in the USA 2001 by
SEVERN HOUSE PUBLISHERS INC., of
595 Madison Avenue, New York, NY 10022.

*A limited edition of 600 copies only was published
by Ash Tree Press in 1999 in Canada only.*

British Library Cataloguing in Publication Data

Aycliffe,   Jonathan,   1949-
    The talisman
    1.Demonology - Fiction
    2.Suspense fiction
    3.Horror tales
    I. Title
    823.9'14 [F]

ISBN 0-7278-5696-0

Printed and bound in Great Britain by
MPG Books Ltd, Bodmin, Cornwall.

INTRODUCTION

Introduction

The Talisman is, in many ways, a departure from my earlier writing under the Aycliffe name. It leans more towards horror than to the ghost story, and I must confess that it was written partly in response to a publisher's suggestion that I target a more youthful audience. Whether it actually will appeal to younger readers remains to be seen; but I don't think my older readers need worry that the story is any less effective because I chose to write with a younger audience in mind.

For one thing, I have from time to time employed elements of physical or semi-physical horror in some of my ghost stories (notably *Naomi's Room* and *The Matrix*). For another, this is not my first departure from the ghost story formula (see *The Lost*). As M.R. James demonstrated so brilliantly, there is no hard and fast demarcation between the two genres (and by one interpretation, you might say he never wrote a proper ghost story in his life).

There are ghosts in *The Talisman*, lots of them, in fact. And there is horror of the sort that owes not a little to *The Exorcist*. I have trawled the past to demonstrate the depth of ancient evil. If Satan originated anywhere, it must have been in Babylon. With a Satanic presence, we know where we stand from the start of the narrative: the normal ambiguity of ghosts is abolished, replaced in some measure by the figure of Adam, the child through whom the evil is largely channelled.

Be assured that the Babylonian bits (for the most part) are accurate, as are the Arabic and Persian references. I share with James the tendency to give in to temptation and provide my readers with authentic incantations and historic personages. I like to think it makes the unbelievable a little bit believeable. And maybe someone, pronouncing the words correctly, will conjure up our worst fears and unleash yet another plague on our heads. Mosquitos in New York today, the flies of Beelzebub in Bloomsbury tomorrow.

Jonathan Aycliffe
Newcastle Upon Tyne
September 1999

THE TALISMAN

Prologue

Baghdad,
The fifth day of the month of Safar in the year 318 from the emigration of the Prophet, corresponding to the ninth day of March in the year 930 of the Christian calendar.

In the Name of God, the Merciful, the Compassionate. Praise be to God, Lord of all the Worlds.

I have looked upon the face of Satan. Let me set this down before anything is forgotten, that others may know and understand, and that the evil I have seen may be averted, if it be God's will.

My name is Abdullah the son of Isa, vazir to his Excellency, the Caliph of the Muslims, Sultan of the Empire of Islam, al-Muqtadir, may God prolong his life and grant him paradise. My parents were Christians, but in my youth I embraced the true faith and entered the school for scribes in Basra. On reaching manhood, I came here to the Abode of Peace and was enrolled among the scribes of the vaziral palace and soon after came to the attention of the lady Shaghab, who is now Queen Mother.

I am now fifty-three years of age, and my hair and beard have grown grey, but until today I was never afraid of death. Now, I recoil from it, as a child from the dark, or a bird from fire. I fear God, but I fear Azrail, the angel of death, even more.

Ten days ago, my Nubian slave Bilal came for me shortly after I had recited the dawn prayers. I was then in the seventh courtyard of my palace. The first rays of the sun were climbing over the east bank of the Tigris, like gold melting in a coiner's vat. I remember it as though from a great distance, as if all that happened, happened a long time ago.

He whispered into my ear, bending low while I sat on the edge of the pool, watching the early light draw patterns on the still water. I

3

nodded wearily, sensing no danger in what he said. It was a day like any other: the sun had risen as on any other day, I had recited my prayers faultlessly, as I had done since I first reached the age of responsibility, Bilal had come to me as he came every day, with the first tidings of the city and its people. I thought nothing was amiss. How easily may we be misled in this life.

He told me the *shurta* had arrested a group of fourteen heretics shortly after midnight, that the men were being kept in the dungeon of the Hasani palace and the women—who numbered five, all of them reputedly of very great beauty—in the New Prison at the Qarar. The Chief Qadi had already issued instructions for the first depositions to be made next month. But first it was necessary for those of us most intimately concerned in the matter to visit the place where the condemned had been known to assemble for their worship of the devil.

I asked Bilal where this might be, thinking it somewhere in the city itself, but he told me it was a week's journey, a distance of twelve farsakhs to the south, to an old city that lies in ruins: Babil, that the Christians call Babylon. When he told me this, my heart shook within me, for I had heard the name many times from my father. It is mentioned in the holy books of the Jews and Christians as a place of great evil and infamy.

Of the journey there I shall say little. The road passes through desolate country empty of inhabitants, where only wild beasts and madmen venture. The few villages we passed were wretched, their people sunk in misery. We were a party of ten, accompanied by guards and servants, making fifty or more in all, yet I confess I felt afraid. It was not that I expected bandits or rebels so close to the capital. But the nearer we drew to the ruined city, the darker grew the sky and the bleaker the countryside. At night, we pitched our tents in open country, taking refuge in God from the perils of the darkness.

We made slow progress, for the roads in those parts are poorly kept, and our animals were weak after the winter. On the ninth day, we came at last to Babylon, nestling near a bend of a small river that is a tributary of the Euphrates. For a moment, seeing its walls in the distance, I thought we had come upon a true city, for all that I knew there could be no city of men in that wilderness. My next thought was that it might be a city of the jinn, inhabited by a race of demons, its walls the work of magic, its houses built of smoke. But as we drew near I saw all this was an illusion. Babylon's great towers had fallen long ago, its gates had crumbled, and its ramparts lay in tatters. We came to the largest of the gates in a great silence, broken only by the rise and fall of our camels' hooves and the jingling of their bridles.

On the advice of Ibn Mujahid the Qur'an reciter, we left the slaves and bodyguard beyond the walls, and entered on foot. There were matters here, he said, that the common people should know nothing of, lest they come to question the faith of God and spread sedition among their fellows. I thought him over-cautious at the time, but no longer. My own faith has been tested, and I fear I may never sleep properly again.

There was a guide with us by the name of Salman, a Persian, a dwarf with a face marked by smallpox. During the journey he had kept to himself, even praying apart from the other servants. I was suspicious of him, and I think with cause. He it was who brought the *shurta* to the house of the heretics in Baghdad, and I am told he had betrayed many to the authorities. He is paid money for his services, but I believe him tainted by the heresies with which he comes in contact. When we return to the city, I shall have him arrested and questioned on his own account.

The gate through which he led us was flanked by the coloured images of false gods, some in the form of bulls, others shaped as creatures I did not recognize. We kept our eyes averted from these idols, but I know that my heart was beating uncomfortably as our steps took us further inside the first enclosure.

On every side we saw the signs of ruination. It was even as God has written in the Qur'an, concerning the Overturned Cities and Iram of the Lofty Pillars: 'We destroyed them and their people, all of them. Behold their dwellings, all in ruins for the evil that they did.'

What evil was done in that place? I smelled it the moment we set foot inside. He sensed it too, the guide Salman, I could see it in his eyes. I stumbled over rubble and reached out for the man next to me, Ahmad al-Tustari. He steadied me, but when I looked into his eyes, I could sense the fear in them.

Salman brought us to a low archway, the only one still standing. In its upper part was carved a symbol that I did not recognize: seven stars set beside a dragon. On the other side of the archway a great slab had been moved aside to reveal steps leading downwards into the earth. We all hung back at first, but the dwarf explained that the purpose of our journey lay here, in an underground chamber. I nodded in acquiescence. Torches were brought and lit, and Salman handed them round.

The steps were ancient and very worn, and we could only climb down one at a time. The dwarf went first, and I followed him, being the chief of those present. A dark smell came from below, like decay, but mingled with other, more recent perfumes, as though incense had been burned there recently. At the foot of the steps a narrow corridor continued beneath the earth for several spans: the dwarf walked upright along it, but I was forced to bend, holding my torch out in front of me. From the walls, the painted figures of demons stared down. I recited prayers for protection, seeking refuge in God from the devil.

Finally we came to a chamber with a high ceiling. This room was circular in form, and was not unlike the warm room of some public baths in the city, except that this was cold and damp, and painted with the figures of ancient devils. The figures were faded and had crumbled away in places, but in spite of that they made me uneasy, for their eyes had a semblance of life in them, and their mouths were open, as though they were on the point of speech.

On the floor at one end of the room lay several corpses.

'Come close,' whispered Salman, and I noticed for the first time that he too was frightened. 'You will be asked of this in the trial.'

I followed him to where the bodies lay in a tangled heap. Behind us I could hear the sounds of my companions entering the chamber. The flickering lights of their torches cast strange shadows on the walls, and at moments it seemed as if the figures painted there strove to come alive.

The bodies were old and shrivelled, and when I looked closely I saw they were the remains of children of varying ages.

'They brought them here from the burial grounds of Wasit and Basra,' said Salman. He was shaking. I could see the fear written on his face. I wondered how he knew this.

'For what purpose?'

'To make them live again.'

'Only God can give life,' I said.

He shook his head.

'Satan gives life,' he whispered. 'Whether it is life or the semblance of life, who can say? But I have seen corpses walk. And I have heard dead men speak, though in tongues I do not understand.'

By this time the others had assembled in the chamber with us. We examined the corpses, and Ibn Mujahid prayed over them, reciting the *fatiha* and the *salat al-mayyit*, as was fitting. When this was done, I turned to Salman.

'I think we have seen all we need to here. Are there other chambers beyond this?'

He looked at me like one who hesitates to speak in the presence of the Caliph, for fear a word out of place may cost him his head or the lives of his children.

'Well?' I asked. 'What holds your tongue? Speak if you value your life.'

'There is another room,' he said. 'A smaller room than this.'

Still he hesitated.

'Yes?'

'Is . . . is this not enough?'

I shook my head, growing angry with him. If we were to execute these rebels, we needed whatever evidence we could find. There have been riots over the price of bread. The Sufis and the Carmathians spread their heresies everywhere. There is unrest at the heart of the empire. When men are restless, they cast aside truth and obedience.

'What is this place,' I asked, 'that you are so afraid of it?'

He tried to look away from me, but I held him fast and would not let him go until he answered.

'It is the realm of ghosts,' he said. 'I dare go no further.'

'Ghosts? What ghosts?'

'The spirits of the dead and the undead.'

'Show me.'

He fell trembling to my feet, and though I threatened him with punishment, he would not move. It was then that Hasan al-Wasiti, Chief of the Upright Witnesses, drew my attention to a doorway in the wall opposite.

'Through here,' he said. 'I think we should look.'

It was a wooden door, very ancient, perhaps as old as the city itself. My hand shook as I took hold of its handle. God forgive me, but I know now I should have listened to the promptings of my heart and left that place at once.

I opened the door. Hasan came forwards and lifted his torch.

Dimly, I could see another chamber, smaller than the one we were in. Bracing myself, I stepped inside. Not for a moment did I consider that anyone else should go before me; I was the highest in rank, it was my responsibility to enter first. But God knows I did not enter that place willingly.

It was a small room, such that only three or four men might enter it comfortably at one time. The ceiling was low, forcing me to bend my head slightly as I stood at its centre. The walls were of brick, unpainted, and appearing much older than those of the chamber from which I had just come.

I raised my torch, and as I did so drew in my breath sharply. Facing me from a low platform in front of the wall opposite was a statue. Even now, my hand trembles as I write of it. It was as tall as a youth, with a man's body and the head of a horned beast. Great black wings rose from its curved shoulders. I needed no one to tell me its name. Iblis. The Great Satan in all his foulness. I shut my eyes and began to turn.

As I did so, I heard a sound behind me, a sound that made the hairs stand upon the back of my head, so out of place and unexpected was it. It was a child's laugh, perfectly distinct and unmistakable. I looked round in bewilderment, but could see nothing other than the statue. The laugh came again, and I turned to Hasan, who still stood in the opening. He did not answer, but when I looked in his eyes I could see that he too had heard it.

I joined him in the doorway and prepared to close the door. At the last moment, I looked back and saw once more the horned figure of Iblis, and by its side a second figure, a small boy dressed all in white, his hair bound with a fillet of silver. He was pale, and his eyes shone strangely. He wore a long white robe, like the Sabaeans of Basra. I staggered back into Hasan's arms.

'Shut the door!' I cried. Even as he did so, I heard another sound—a dry rustling, like the rustling of wings.

We shall not return to Babylon. When we are safely in Baghdad again, I shall write an edict forbidding all, be they Muslim, Jew, or Christian, to enter that place, on the pain of death. Before we left, I instructed the captain of the bodyguard to break the earth above that accursed chamber, and to fill it with sand until there was no more to be seen of it. No one shall ever set foot in there again.

Chapter One

The days are drawing in again, and the nights seem to last for ever. Autumn this year is more mist than mellow fruitfulness. I see myself reflected in the windows of strangers, a pale man walking past their houses, snatching a glimpse of their felicity, stealing a crumb of comfort from the sight of warm open fires, flickering televisions, soft-shaded lamps. Then I pass on and am swallowed up by evening. Next month there will be Christmas trees and fairy lights and jolly Santas. The festive season. The season of goodwill. I cannot bear to think of it.

Nicola and I arrived in London at the end of autumn that year, each trailing a former life, each eager for what lay ahead. We had been married six months. She used to cup her hands and hold them steady in front of her face, like a Muslim at prayer, and I would hold them and bring them to my cheeks, and her fingers would move gently over me, like a kitten's paws. She'd gone blind fifteen years earlier, long before we met. It hurt me that she might never know what I looked like, but she said her fingers read me as if they were eyes, and she liked what she saw. She was always a flatterer.

Like me, her son Adam had never known his mother any other way. She'd brought him up almost single-handed, fed him, bathed him, sent him off to school every day with a packed lunch, not caring about the darkness that surrounded her more heavily than any autumn mist or January fog. He was six when we met, a quiet boy, intelligent, but cautious of his intellect. He could read more rapidly in Braille than on the printed page. If need be, he could pick his way through a crowded room in darkness. The children of the blind are often like that, I'm told. Had she put the darkness in him while he was still in the womb, given him her compensations and her fears?

He took to me slowly and reluctantly, like a dog that has been in quarantine so long it cannot remember its own master. No, that's unfair, I never sought to own Adam; he belonged entirely to himself. But he had been close to Nicola for so long, had combed her hair, made her meals, and watched her lighting candles with a tremulous hand so often it was no surprise that he resented me at first. I had to win him, and that took time.

Of her first husband, she would not speak. He had abandoned her soon after Adam was born, a few years into her blindness. No excuse, no explanation. Did Adam have his father's looks, I asked? She didn't know, she'd never seen the boy, but, yes, people who'd known her husband said they were alike. He'd been an Arab, Khalil—that much I discovered. An Iraqi, a refugee from Saddam's regime. They'd met while they were both students. She'd been reading history, he was a scientist, what kind I'm not sure. A physicist, probably: the Iraqis produce physicists like we produce commodity brokers.

I wasn't really all that interested in Khalil. I'd fallen for Nicola, and her past was unimportant. The first time I saw her, she'd come to a lecture I was giving on late Sumerian burial customs. Not exactly riveting stuff, but thirty people had turned out on a dirty February evening to immerse themselves in it. I was teaching at Manchester then, on a temporary contract I'd landed soon after getting back from eastern Turkey.

I remember nothing now of the lecture. Nor, I suspect, does anyone else. What I do remember vividly is Nicola coming to me afterwards, to ask questions I was ill-equipped to answer. I'd noticed her all through the talk, I'd hardly been able to take my eyes off her, and every time I tried to look elsewhere I'd found my gaze straying back to that strangely lovely face.

Her white stick took me completely by surprise. Nothing in her posture or expression had alerted me to her blindness. I took her for coffee, just the two of us and her guide dog, and I fell in love. Not the dull, routine falling in love I'd experienced five or six times in my life before, but a dazzling, consternating plunge, like someone who opens a hidden door to find himself, not in a new room, but a new world entirely, with its own earth and sea and sky.

It took her longer, months longer. I like to think she'd have been smitten at once if she could have seen my face. But perhaps not. I remember the first time she touched my face with those gently probing fingers. It wasn't like being looked at. Nor was it the mere touching of a sighted woman. Her fingers grazed my skin, but as they moved I felt them penetrate to the very depths of me.

After that she kissed me for the first time. Gravely, almost demurely in the first instants, her lips, then her tongue gaining confidence only slowly, and then, their first tentative enquiries done, taking my mouth with more passion than I had ever known. I think I entered a little into her darkness then. And drew back, frightened and sad. When she kissed me, she closed her eyes. Later, when we made love for the first time, she insisted I turn out the lights. She saw with her skin, and in the darkness I became her pupil.

We lived together in Manchester for about a year before deciding to marry. The year was essential: it took Adam at least that long to come to terms with me. I would have been content to go on just as we were, but she wanted marriage, and I acquiesced. It had something to do with Khalil. Until she married me, she said, she couldn't feel entirely free of him. I didn't want his ghost around either, so I went out one autumn morning and bought a ring, the most expensive I could afford.

A week after the wedding I was told that my temporary contract with the university would not be renewed. That same day I heard there was a post available in London, at the British Museum, with a five-year contract and the strong possibility of renewal.

We arrived in London on a sunny day at the end of October. We had arranged to stay with friends until we could find a place of our own. The leaves had started to turn, and all along the street bright trees of gold and copper waited patiently for winter. Our first days in the city were suffused by a coral light that fell unevenly through our windows at dusk. I described it to Nicola, watching night fall across the roofs of the houses opposite, and she held my hand and whispered her love for me in the silence of sunset.

She remembered trees in autumn, and pink light, and darkness descending slowly. She had gone blind at sixteen, suddenly, between one breath and the next, in the middle of a French lesson at school. One moment the world had been laid in front of her like a prize, the next it had been snatched away. She'd wanted to be a photographer.

We spent our evenings and weekends looking at a succession of flats and houses in different parts of London. Some were too pricey, others were awkwardly situated, and almost all of them required extensive work to let Nicola move around without bumping her head or cracking her shins.

A month and more passed, and though our friends said nothing, we knew it wouldn't be long before we outstayed our welcome. I mentioned the problem to one of my new colleagues at the museum, and he said he'd make some enquiries. That was how it began. If there'd been time to consider, to look round further . . . But there wasn't time, and the truth is it seemed a heaven-sent opportunity.

Terry Forbes, my colleague, came back to me a week later, a broad grin creasing his usually placid features.

'I've got the very thing for you, Tom' he said. 'It's cheap, it's in Bloomsbury, and it isn't on the open market yet.'

'It's got a leaking roof.'

He shook his head.

'What, then? No roof?'

He laughed and shook his head again.

'You'll need a surveyor to check the place out. But as far as I know there isn't a catch. Have you ever heard of Peter Lazenby?'

'The Arabist?'

'That's right. He used to teach at London University. Retired in nineteen sixty-something.'

'I didn't know he was still alive.'

'That's just the point. He isn't. Peter died a few months ago. After his retirement he stayed on in his old house in Gordon Square. Never moved out. He used to drop in here regularly. Archaeology was his passion. Mesopotamia mostly—your sort of thing.'

'I didn't know that. So what's this got to do with my house-hunting?'

'Well, Peter left a lot of his books and papers to the Museum. I went over to Gordon Square yesterday, just to make a rough inventory, see what was worth keeping. His solicitor was there, a man called Beamish. I just happened to ask what was happening to the house. Lazenby was in his nineties when he died, and his wife Miriam popped her clogs years ago. I wondered if there were any children or grandchildren.'

'And?'

'Apparently not. The estate belongs to the Society for Mesopotamian Studies, and they've decided to put the house up for sale. Beamish said that if you got in now with an offer you might strike lucky. The Society wants a quick sale.'

We went round that evening. Terry had spoken to Beamish, and the solicitor showed us round himself. A stuffy man with a ginger moustache that had been trimmed the way some people trim hedges, as though it represented an art form. He simpered when I was introduced as 'Doctor Alton', and fussed over Nicola as though she was made of tissue paper.

The house was untidy and in need of redecoration. It hadn't seen paint in thirty years or more, and every surface that was capable of attracting dust had collected a small mountain of the stuff. The furniture had probably been bought by Lazenby after he got married. But, stuffed as it still was with the old man's books and papers, filled as it was with mementoes of a long and active life, the house won me to its heart within minutes. I could not resist it. I felt a need for it that grew to a dull ache as Beamish conducted me from room to room, and I felt a terrible anxiety that the asking price would be beyond our means. I wanted the house, and I almost could have believed it wanted me.

Nicola followed us, seeing nothing, but running her hands over everything. We were on the second floor when she turned to Beamish.

'Someone blind has lived here, haven't they?' she said. 'The way the furniture's laid out. And no sharp corners anywhere.'

Beamish looked at her in surprise.

'Didn't you know?' he asked.

'Know what?'

'Why, Professor Lazenby was blind for twenty years and more. After his wife died they thought he wouldn't be able to manage on his own. But a housekeeper came in during the day, and he stayed on. You'll find the house very safe, Mrs Alton. Very safe indeed.'

Chapter Two

'Tom? Is that you?'

I knew when I answered the phone that the voice was familiar, but I couldn't place it at first.

'Who's this?'

'Come on, Tom—don't you remember your old friends?'

'Ed! Ed Monelli. What the hell are you up to? Where are you?'

'I'm in London. I got in this morning.'

I hadn't seen Ed in—what was it?—six or seven years. We'd worked together on digs in Iran and Turkey, then I'd come back to England to teach and he'd stayed out in the Middle East running archaeological expeditions for one American institute after another. His wife Caroline was one of my favourites: smart, good-looking (too good-looking), tough. She'd pulled us out of more than one tight spot in the old days.

'How'd you get my number? I've only been here a couple of months.'

'People talk. I hear you're the new chief honcho in the museum's Mesopotamian section.'

'Not quite that, but close. Is that why you're ringing?'

'Hell, no. You're almost family. But I'd like us to meet up. You doing anything special for lunch?'

'Looks like I am now.'

We had lunch at the Museum Street Café. Ed was paying. American money and a generous nature. I knew he wanted something from me. Outside, the first snow of winter fell, stinted at first, then suddenly lavish, swirling through the air like a million white butterflies. I watched it fall as Ed talked. Ed, never Curt, not even to his friends. He was a small man, dark-haired and bearded, a little like a gnome gone right. The backs of his hands were peppered with fine black hairs that vanished into his sleeve and continued, for all I

15

knew, across his entire body. The trick lay in his smile. It lit him up, transforming his Saturnine looks to those of an angel. But it wasn't there. The smile he gave me was no more than a pale ghost, flickering for a moment on his lips before vanishing back into whatever dark hole he'd called it up from.

He seemed sombre, a mood I did not associate with him. I told him a little about my new job, and said I'd just been married. We talked for a while about that. Then, in a moment of thickening snow, I asked after Caroline.

'Isn't she in London with you?'

I saw his face change, and I think I guessed what he would say long before he actually spoke.

'Caroline's dead,' he said, his voice very nearly a whisper, though the words carried to me without any loss of clarity.

'Dead?'

'Two months ago. I've only just . . . I've not told many people yet. You must forgive me. I should have thought . . .'

His voice was near breaking, but he rallied himself and downed a glass of red wine in a couple of swallows, refilling it at once.

'How did she . . .? How did it happen?' I asked. I was already convinced she'd died in an accident, so hard was it for me to imagine Caroline seriously ill. She could not have let herself simply fade from life, of that I was certain.

'We were on a dig together, working at a gate foundation. Caroline was just across from me. She stood up to get something and staggered. Said she felt faint. I told her to go and lie down. She went to our tent. That must have been about nine o'clock. I went on working till just before noon. When I went to the tent to check on her, she was dead.'

'Good God. Was there . . .?'

He nodded, understanding me.

'Yes, they did an autopsy. A local doctor, but he'd been trained in the States. Knew his stuff. Said it was some sort of embolism. Even if she'd been rushed straight to hospital, it's unlikely her life could have been saved.'

'How dreadful. To have so little warning.'

'It's how Caroline would have wanted it. Quick and relatively painless. She hated the idea of a lingering death.'

'How old was she?'

'Forty-one.' He looked at me. 'God, I miss her,' he said. They'd been married almost twenty years. The snow continued falling, unaware of grief or happiness.

We talked a little longer about Caroline, about times we'd all spent together. Too few memories, and each too short.

'Are you in London for any special reason?' I asked finally.

'Well, we shut the dig down for the winter, and I've nothing to take me back to Chicago right now. To tell you the truth, I'd planned on spending the winter just roaming round Europe. Don't feel like seeing folks back home just yet.'

'You could stay with us while you're in London,' I said. 'If you don't mind putting up with some disorder. We're having the place done up a little.'

'That's fine with me. More than fine. I'd like to stay, get to know your wife.'

'You'll like the house. It's a bit run down, but it has atmosphere. The last owner lived in it for over fifty years. Actually, you probably know of him. A man called Peter Lazenby. The one who wrote that book on Babylonian social structures.'

A frown creased his forehead.

'Lazenby? That's curious. While I was . . .'

He was about to say something more when there was a call behind him, and Alan Waterstone, my boss, strode towards us. We hadn't planned things that way, but he'd heard Ed was in town and was keen to see him. We chatted for a while, and Ed and Alan made arrangements to meet. When Alan had gone, Ed and I continued talking about our personal affairs, catching up on old friends, swapping gossip about people we scarcely knew. When the bill came, Ed insisted on paying.

'Consider this business,' he said. 'As a matter of fact, you're the man I came here to see.'

'Me personally, or me professionally?'

'Both. I'm seeing you personally now, but tomorrow, I plan to call on you at the museum. I've got something I'd like you to see. Well, photographs anyway. The real thing hasn't arrived in London yet.'

'You intrigue me.'

'I don't mean to, but it's something I'd rather you didn't mention to anyone else at the moment. Oddly enough, it's connected to

Caroline. It was her last major find. She dug it up about a week before she died.'

'You haven't even told me where this was.'

'The dig? Didn't I say? We got permission to go back this year. We were at Babylon, Tom. That's where Caroline died. And that's where this thing comes from.'

Chapter Three

Nicola was waiting for me with good news when I got home that night. She'd found a job working with blind teenagers at a community centre ten minutes away. All that day she'd been out, getting to know the route there and back. The job started in a week's time.

'It's perfect, darling,' she said as I hugged and congratulated her. 'I work three days a week, which gives me plenty of time for Adam and working on my thesis.'

She was writing a doctoral thesis on Hammurabi. When I had time, I taped books and articles for her, and I was learning Braille in order to type out materials she could use. She expected no concessions on account of her infirmity, but research work without sight is laborious. I used to joke that she'd married me for my books and my knowledge of the field, and she used to laugh and shake her head.

'I married you for your voice,' she would say. And she was perfectly serious. Voices were her way to people. She knew my moods before I was aware of them myself, just by listening to me speak.

I told her about Ed, and said I'd asked him to stay. She was a little put out that I hadn't bothered to ask her first, but when she discovered who he was, her objections evaporated.

'I'd love to meet him. Is he in London alone?'

I explained about Caroline.

'You loved her, didn't you?' she said.

'Yes, a little. But she and Ed were so close there was never any chance for someone else. How'd you know?'

'Your voice,' she said, smiling, and drawing me to her, as though Caroline's death had freed part of me for her and made me more completely hers. Adam was in his room doing his homework, but we sneaked off to bed anyway. When she was naked, I caressed her for a long time, stroking and kissing her, giving her back what sight denied.

Ed arrived in my office the next day as arranged. The sombre mood had not left him, and this time something had been added to it, an emotion just out of my reach.

'Tom,' he said, as he settled into the chair opposite me, 'I was over the moon when I heard you'd taken over this outfit.'

'That's putting it a bit strongly. I told you. . . .'

'Forget what you told me. For my purposes you're in charge. I don't go to anybody else. And I was over the moon because I knew there was someone in this place I could trust. I can trust you, can't I, Tom?'

'Provided whatever it is is legal, yes.'

'It's legal, but it may not be popular. I managed to squeeze a permit out of the Iraqis to ship Caroline's find out here. It's due to arrive at Heathrow tomorrow morning.'

'How the hell did you manage that?'

'They're going through a religious phase. This thing belongs to the pagan past, and they want nothing to do with it. I'm doing them a favour.'

Light spilled through my window, thick with mist. I saw dust rise in thin spirals, as though some quality of the light created it. It was an old room, full of ghosts. Or so I quaintly liked to think at the time. Of course, I knew nothing then. Of ghosts, or what they trail behind them.

'What is this thing?'

'I'll come to that. Caroline found it in a chamber we stumbled on, not far from the Ishtar Gate. The area had been excavated before, but no one had noticed that part of it had been filled in much later than the rest. Caroline discovered signs of wreckage, as though it had been done deliberately, and not that many centuries ago. We dug down and found a couple of rooms, one large circular chamber, and a smaller one. That's where we found the statue. And that's not all we found. There were bones all round it. Human bones. Children's bones. Fifteen or sixteen skeletons.'

I shuddered. Ed and Caroline had never had children, perhaps that made him insensitive. But I thought of Adam, and the children Nicola and I planned to have in the future.

'A Babylonian statue,' I said. 'That's a rare find. Caroline must have been pleased.'

'She was. At first. After she saw the whole thing, I don't know. For one thing, it certainly isn't Babylonian. And it doesn't look Sumerian, Akkadian, or Assyrian. Except . . .'

His voice tailed off. Something was troubling him, and again I caught a whiff of that emotion he was making such efforts to repress.

'You mean it was put there later?'.

He shook his head.

'I don't know. I don't think so. There's an inscription. I haven't deciphered it all yet: I thought you might lend a hand. But one thing's sure: it's in Old Babylonian.'

'I don't suppose you have any photographs of this statue.'

'In a manner of speaking,' he said. He pulled a packet of photographs from the inside pocket of his jacket.

'I had these developed yesterday,' he said. 'A drugstore called Boots. They any good?'

'Good enough,' I said. 'I'd say they were reliable.'

'That's what I thought. Here, take a look.'

I opened the packet and tipped its contents onto my desk. There were thirty-six prints in all, plus negatives. Every one of them was black. I examined the negatives: they were identical. Putting the pictures back in the wallet, I passed them to Ed without a word.

'Somebody must have forgotten to take the lens cap off,' I said.

'Looks that way. But all is not lost. Caroline made a drawing the day after we unearthed it. This is a copy.'

He passed me a sheet of paper. It showed a statue, all black, sketched in charcoal. A man with the head of a horned beast. The drawing conveyed more than any photograph might have done. It seemed almost alive. The eyes in particular had a vibrancy about them that may not have been in the original stone. They stared out at me from the page, as though animated by some malign intelligence.

'Not very pretty, is he?' I pushed the paper back across the desk.

'Not pretty, no. But a major find. What do you think?'

'I can see why you're excited. I've never seen anything quite like it. Not Babylonian, as you say. But with a Babylonian inscription.'

'Do you think you'd have room for him? Here in the museum?'

I looked at him, puzzled. The dust motes swirled in the light, as though trapped there, fragile things behind glass. Not far away, in the public rooms, visitors moved to and fro, intent on the past. They walked like ghosts past the remains of other men, thinking for a few brief moments of their lives, then left to buy their hamburgers in the cafeteria, their souvenirs in the museum.

'Why here? Surely your expedition was American. One of your own museums . . . Chicago, the Metropolitan, maybe Penn State . . .'

He shook his head briefly and precisely.

'They won't take it. I don't need to ask. You've seen the drawing. We've got a lot of crazy people where I come from. They get upset about fairy stories in children's books. Cinderella is occultism. Robert Mapplethorpe with horns was a Satanic plot. Put this fellow in a public museum and you can bet on trouble. I'd feel a lot safer if he was here.'

I hesitated only moments. After all, it was an exciting find, and it would consolidate my position at the museum if I succeeded in adding such a treasure to their collections so soon after my appointment. I could already feel that second contract in my grasp.

'It won't be my decision,' I said.

'You can tell them how important it is. They won't hesitate.'

'What about the Iraqi authorities? Our trustees won't be happy about storing up trouble for the future. This Elgin Marbles business . . .'

He shook his head.

'I told you, that's been taken care of. The papers are all in order.'

'I'll take your word for it. When do I get to see the real thing?'

'Why don't you come out to the airport with me tomorrow morning? The plane arrives at ten fifteen.'

I looked at my diary.

'Yes, that's fine. Now, I told Nicola you'd be home for dinner. Your bedroom's been aired and dusted. And wait till I tell you who slept there last.'

He picked up the wallet of dud photographs, and as he did so, one fell out onto the desk top. I glanced down as he retrieved it. The black had started to fade, as though affected by exposure to the light, and in the top left-hand corner a shape had started to appear, fragmentary and indistinct. The next moment Ed had replaced it in the wallet and returned it to his pocket. I put it down to a trick of the light and went on with my story.

Chapter Four

I arrived home a little later than usual the following evening. Ed and I had been out to the airport as planned and had brought the statue back home. I'd had to spend the rest of the day at work. When I got back, the statue was still in the crate in which it had been shipped. They were all waiting for me to arrive—Ed, Nicola, and young Adam—before opening it. The crate had been carried upstairs to the room behind the stairs and placed in the spot where the statue was to reside during its time in the house. I flung my coat on the newel post and followed the others.

We made rather a ceremony of it. Glasses of red wine—and one of ginger cordial—were poured, Ed made a little speech, I gratefully acknowledged receipt of the artefact, and, quite unrehearsed and perfectly genuine, Nicola invoked the spirit of Peter Lazenby to watch over the strange object that had travelled so many miles to enter his home. I often wondered afterwards what prompted her to do that. It may have been nothing more than an attempt at wit. Yet, in the light of what happened, I cannot think that was all.

Ed had already loosened the nails, and it was the work of a few moments to remove them entirely and lift aside the front section of the crate. Wads of packing followed, and then, like a diver emerging suddenly from great depths, the statue stood before us.

The artist who had created him had shown a skill far in advance of any I had seen in Mesopotamian work before. There was something simultaneously stylized and yet lifelike about the little figure—he came only to my chest—as though it had been carved from imagination tempered by experience. Though the head was that of a beast, the whole effect was that of a human being in disguise. The malign intelligence that I had seen in the eyes had not been a mere accident of Caroline's drawing: it was there in the original as well, magnified by the dense black stone out of which the figure had been carved.

'His name is Shabbatil,' said Ed, almost in awe. 'You'll see it carved on the inscription on the base.'

'I've never heard of a god by that name before,' I said.

'You can check it for yourself later; but Caroline was pretty confident about the reading.'

Nicola stepped forward.

'May I touch him?'

Ed nodded.

'We'll take away the rest of the packing first, then you'll have room.'

The crate came apart easily. We cleared away the wood and wadding, and Nicola approached the statue cautiously. Adam stood a little behind her, watching. Her hands reached out, and she took the figure by the shoulders and slowly started to run her fingers over it. I saw her shiver once or twice. When she reached the face, her hands slowed further, inching their way across the cold black surface of the stone; and I knew she was seeing it as surely as she saw my face when she stroked it, as surely as she saw Adam's face. At last, her hands fell away, dropping to her side. She stood like that, for a minute or so, face to face with the statue, then spoke without turning her face to me.

'It's old,' she said. 'Very old. Much older than Babylon. Older than Akkad. Older than Sumer.'

I had never known her speak like this before. Not for a moment did I doubt what she said. There was a confidence in her voice that could not be challenged.

'I don't understand,' I said. 'How can you tell?'

She turned her face to me then, and I sensed that something was troubling her.

'There's a lot about me you don't know, Tom,' she said. Without another word, she turned and left the room. Adam followed her. I looked at Ed, and saw him frown and shake his head. In the dim light of the little room, the statue seemed almost to glow with its own ancient darkness.

Later that evening, Ed set up a camera and took more photographs of Shabbatil. He still did not properly understand what had blacked out all the roll Caroline had exposed in Iraq, but suspected the x-ray machines at the airport, or perhaps the equipment at Boots. He had almost finished when I came in to say it was time for supper.

'I've used up most of this roll,' he said, 'but there must be half a dozen shots left. Why don't I take a few shots of you all with the statue?'

We came in dutifully, and one by one he photographed us side by side with Shabbatil. I returned the compliment, and we went off for a late meal of pasta and salad, followed by round upon round of cinnamon toast. It was good having Ed to stay. He was an unintrusive guest, the sort who makes himself part of the family and yet never seems to be there when not wanted.

All through the meal, Nicola was subdued. My attempts to cheer her up were met, not by any rebuff or frostiness, but by uncertain smiles that strayed across her face for a few seconds and slipped away again.

We were wakened at three that morning by a cry from Adam's room. I slid out of bed, shivering in the sudden winter chill.

'I'll see to him, it's all right. He's probably had a nightmare.'

When I reached his room, he was bolt upright in bed. A night-light burned beside him, as it always did through the dark hours. A glass that always sat on his bedside table lay overturned, the milk that had been in it spilled in a white pool on the floor.

'What's wrong?' I asked. 'Did you have a bad dream?'

He shook his head.

'Did something frighten you?'

He nodded, still unable to speak. Nicola appeared behind me in the open doorway. She made her way to the bed and sat down next to Adam, smoothing his hair back from his forehead and comforting him with whispers. Reassured, he looked up at me.

'A boy,' he said. 'I woke up and he was standing over there.'

He pointed to a spot about three feet away from where I was standing.

'What sort of boy?' asked Nicola.

'A bit bigger than me. He had long hair with something tied round it. He was dressed in white. A long white dress.'

'What was he doing?' I asked.

'Nothing. He was just standing staring at me.'

'You must have been asleep,' said Nicola. 'There's no one there now.'

Adam shook his head vigorously. If I had learned anything about him, it was that he was an honest child, utterly without duplicity. Nicola had taught him from an early age that to lie is to invite disaster: the blind suffer if they do not know the truth. A ten-pound note must be a ten-pound note, not five; a staircase must have seven steps, not eight.

'I was asleep,' he said, 'but I woke up. Something woke me. The boy was laughing. But when I looked at him, he stopped laughing.'

'Well, darling, sometimes we think we're awake when we're not. Would you like to come back to our room and sleep with us for the rest of the night?'

'Yes,' he said. 'Yes, please. I'm frightened here on my own.'

He got out of bed and put his feet into his slippers, huge furry slippers with bears' heads. Nicola took his hand and walked from the room. I remained behind to tidy the bedclothes and switch off the lamp. As I reached the door, I turned. Something was wrong. I could see nothing and hear nothing. But as I made to go, I smelled a faint perfume on the air. Spices. The sort of spices I remember smelling in the suk at Baghdad: cumin, coriander, cinnamon, turmeric, *dukka*. And behind the familiar smells, another, darker smell, something I had never encountered before. The perfume lingered most strongly around the spot where Adam said he had seen the boy. I moved forward and sniffed again, but the smell had gone as if it had never been.

By the next morning, Adam had recovered his spirits. I said nothing to either him or Nicola about the perfume I fancied I had smelled in his room the previous night. He slept until late, and when he woke his memory of waking was hopelessly muddled with other dreams he had had.

We went down to breakfast together. Ed was already in the kitchen, brewing coffee and toasting toast. As I say, the perfect guest. Nicola made an omelette for herself. Ed watched her, fascinated by the skill with which she manoeuvred implements and ingredients as though she could see them.

There was a thud from the hallway, and I went out to pick up my copy of *The Times*. I glanced through the headlines as I walked back to the kitchen. One in particular caught my eye.

'Look at this,' I said, holding the paper out to Ed and pointing to a short article near the bottom of the front page. He read it and looked up at me, frowning.

'You don't think it could be the same one?' he said.

'It's possible.'

An Iraqi airliner had crashed over Greece on a flight from London to Baghdad. Details were still coming in from Athens. But the report contained one piece of information that arrested us. The plane had landed at Heathrow the previous morning, where it had been serviced and refuelled before its return flight. It was the same aeroplane on which the statue of Shabbatil had been flown. Two hundred and seventy people had been on board for the Baghdad flight. It was thought there had been no survivors.

Chapter Five

It was a Saturday, and after breakfast I said I'd take Adam into town to do some Christmas shopping. He'd been looking forward to it for a while, but our house move had made it impossible until now. Nicola still had work to do in preparation for her new job, and Ed had old friends to visit in Hampstead.

I decided to take him down to Covent Garden, and then, as it grew dark, to cut along to Regent Street to see the lights. So preoccupied had I been with my new job and moving house, the brightly-lit Christmas windows and the shops thronged with shoppers came as a surprise. Adam was mesmerized. He'd never been Christmas shopping in London before, never been as aware of the shops as he was that day. Everywhere we went there was something fresh for him to see, something intriguing, something beyond all his previous experience of life. And I began to see the world freshly as well, as though seeing through his eyes. It was a skill he had, one he had honed to perfection by acting as eyes for his mother. He seemed to absorb everything. I knew he would relay every detail to her when he returned: colours, shapes, images, textures, a whole kaleidoscope of Christmas sensations. And I suddenly realized that, when he grew up, he would see the world quite differently to other people.

On the way, we dropped Ed's reel of film off at a camera shop which offered a three-hour developing service.

From time to time, Adam would glance behind him, as though he expected to see someone approaching him.

'Are you all right, Adam?' I asked. 'Have you seen somebody following you?'

He shook his head, but I sensed hesitation even as he did so.

'Are you still frightened after your bad dream last night? Would you like to talk about it?'

Again that cautious shake of the head. I sensed that he wanted to talk, but that something held him back; and I knew that to press him would only silence him completely. Whatever he needed to say he would say in his own time.

We visited a very peculiar Father Christmas in a chocolate shop in Neal Street: his long white beard was almost certainly real, and he spoke with a very odd accent—I pretended to myself that we had stumbled on the genuine article. His face, genial yet somehow hovering on the edge of a very private madness, haunted my sleep for nights to come, until it was thrust out by other madnesses.

We had lunch in the main Covent Garden complex, entertained by buskers. As they danced and played their instruments, something wonderful happened. First, a light snow began to fall, a soft, powdery snow that seemed to dance in time to the music. And then, as though by pre-arrangement, the dancers and musicians stopped, all but one. A girl remained standing, her long blonde hair tied back in a simple tress, her quilted coat buttoned against the cold. She raised a flute to her lips and played Silent Night, and all around her the world fell quiet, and even the traffic seemed hushed. No one moved while she played. It was as if all things conspired in that moment to form the season. Adam listened entranced. And that evening, when he returned home, before anything else he told his mother about the 'beautiful lady in the snow'.

One odd thing happened after that. Adam and I set off to cross the patch of ground between the café and the rear of the square. At that moment, the snow lay perfectly on the ground. We were the first to walk on it. As we reached a spot about half-way across, I noticed Adam turn, as he had done before. I too looked round, thinking someone might be following us: perhaps we had left something behind. But there was no one there. And yet, glancing down at the ground, I could have sworn that, for a moment, the imprints of small feet lay lightly marked on top of the snow. Then the falling snow covered them and started to fill our own footprints.

Regent Street completed the day for Adam. Bright lights enhanced the darkness like stars on a perfect night. Only once did he stumble in his enchantment. I saw him frown and catch his breath.

'What's the matter?' I asked. 'Is something wrong?'

He shook his head from habit, then nodded.

'Mummy can't see any of these things,' he said, 'not ever.'

'She saw them when she was a little girl,' I told him. 'She still remembers. Ask her when you get back. And tell her all about these.'

He brightened a little, but I could see that knowledge of his mother's plight diminished the sighted world for him. I believe he would willingly have sacrificed his own vision to bring her the world again. And, thinking of her in that same moment, I knew I would have done the same.

'Come on,' I said, 'it's time we were going home. Mummy will be missing us.'

We took a taxi back, stopping to pick up the photographs on the way. I opened the packet and glanced through them as we drove the rest of the way back home, wanting to be sure there were no problems this time. This batch had been properly exposed and developed, but for one thing: the statue of Shabbatil appeared in none of them. There was either an empty room, or pictures of Nicola, Adam, and myself. More disturbingly, there were two shots of Nicola on her own. Ed had been standing beside her each time. I know—I had taken them myself.

Nicola seemed fine when we arrived. Her day had gone well, she said, and she'd got through more work than expected. Adam hopped up and down impatiently, bursting to talk about everything he'd seen and done. A huge mushroom risotto was waiting for us in the kitchen.

Adam scarcely ate, so excited was he by our day out. We'd come home laden with bags stuffed with presents, and it was all Adam could do not to blurt out what he had bought. For my part I felt only a certain sadness that he'd been able to leave the bags standing openly in the hallway, knowing they did not have to be hidden from Nicola's gaze.

Throughout the meal, Nicola smiled and laughed as Adam continued his animated chatter, or admonished him for not eating. But every so often she would cast a sideways glance at me, and I sensed that something was troubling her, something she could not mention in front of Adam.

Ed had not yet returned from his friends' house. It had been a vague arrangement, and we reckoned he must be staying to supper there. It was a bit odd, all the same, that he did not ring to let us know.

Adam went to bed a little before nine, protesting but thoroughly exhausted and ready for sleep. His night-light was switched on as usual, and when Nicola kissed him goodnight, she paused for a while, as though praying silently over her little boy. It seemed out of character. Had something happened to make her apprehensive for him?

'Why don't we take him to the Advent Carol Service at St Paul's?' she said as we left the room.

'Yes, that's a good idea. He loved that performance of "Silent Night" today. Even if I don't believe, I'd hate to deny him something so beautiful.'

'Don't you?' she asked. 'Don't you believe?'

'You know I don't,' I replied. 'Not in God, anyway, and not in the Church.'

'Nor I. But I do believe there are forces. Forces for good and . . . forces for evil. I think there must be a devil.'

'With hooves and horns, a bit like old Shabbatil down there?' I smiled, but she did not smile back.

'Perhaps,' she said, 'perhaps.'

We went downstairs. Since living with Nicola, I had all but given up television. Most evenings we listened to the radio. A programme was due on Radio Four about Roman archaeology in Britain. I glanced at my watch.

'Odd that Ed still hasn't got in touch,' I said. 'Have you got a number for his friends?'

She shook her head.

'He didn't leave one. They're probably still at dinner, if they've even started. Who are they anyway? Did he say?'

'Some Americans. Not archaeologists. Not even academics. Business people he knew back in Chicago.'

'Makes a refreshing change.' I looked at her as I bent to switch on a light. She seemed pale. I went to the windows and drew the curtains. It was still snowing outside, more heavily now. I imagined Nicola standing in the empty night, snow settling on her hair like frost on grass. 'What's the matter, love?' I asked. 'You don't seem yourself.'

She found her chair and sat down. For a moment I thought she was going to ignore my question, but she sagged into the chair, abandoning whatever pretence she had intended to display.

'I wish we'd never come to this house,' she said.

'I don't understand. I thought you loved it.'

'It has something in it. I don't know what exactly, but I don't like it. It was there at the beginning, but very faint, I could barely feel it. I thought it had some connection to Lazenby, that it would leave once we moved in. But it didn't go. It's still here. When that statue arrived, it became much stronger. It's here now. It never leaves. And I think it means us harm.'

They found Ed later that night in an alley behind Russell Square tube station. He'd never reached his friends. At first it was thought he'd been killed in a mugging and his body dumped there. But there were no signs of violence on him anywhere, at least not externally. The postmortem discovered the cause of death, but a cause so bizarre that the coroner's court could not reach a verdict. His lungs had been filled with red sand. Desert sand. As if he'd breathed it in and choked on it. I was there, but I said nothing. I'd seen sand like that before. On a dry day one midsummer, far to the south of Baghdad, close to a town called Hilla, on a visit to the fabled ruins of Babylon.

I transferred the statue of Shabbatil to a storeroom in the museum first thing on Monday morning.

Chapter Six

Christmas arrived, and though Ed's death cast a dark shadow over the season, he had never been close enough to Nicola or Adam for it to ruin the festivities for them. The carol concert was the highlight of our year. I think it was then that Adam discovered his vocation. His life would be given over to music. We took the tube back, and as we walked the remainder of the way home, Adam strode between us, his hands in ours, humming softly to himself.

I thought I heard him hum just now, softly, in the next room; but there was no one there. He and the other boy come here more frequently of late. I do what I can to keep out of their way. Last night, he screamed for hours at a stretch. There was a time when I would have gone to him; but not now, not knowing what he has become. And is still becoming. It does not happen all at once. Some of the books say it can take centuries. I can well believe it.

Christmas Day and the days before and after it went by in a delirium of visits and get-togethers. Nicola's parents came down from York, and my mother travelled up from Devon. It was the first time they had all met since the wedding, and, whatever our apprehensions, they got on well together. No more was said of Nicola's fear that there was 'something' in the house, and I put it down to the strain of the move. Being blind and finding herself suddenly in unfamiliar surroundings, she quite naturally inhabited the new house with a presence from her own unconscious. Or so I thought. I was still an unbeliever then: in good, in evil, in the reality and otherness of death.

Ed's belongings remained in his room, two large suitcases, a shoulder bag, and a briefcase. In the New Year, I contacted his department at Chicago University, and they made arrangements to have everything flown back. God knows where it all ended up.

Caroline and his parents were all dead, there were no children. I imagined some drab ending, with all his worldly goods packed up and sent to a charity shop, anonymous and next to worthless.

While packing, I came across a journal open on the desk. He'd been writing in it the night before he died, or perhaps early that morning. I noticed a reference to Shabbatil, and realized the journal might contain useful information on the statue, for which I now felt a personal responsibility. Dutifully, I contacted Ed's departmental head, a man called Ashby. Professor Ashby was an Englishman who had strayed across the Atlantic fifteen or so years earlier and was now America's foremost authority on Egyptian hieratic script. I'd met him a couple of times at conferences, and he had no hesitation in letting me hold on to the journal until I had gleaned any salient information from it. I said I'd send it on later. I never did.

I didn't get the chance to read the journal right away, however. No sooner had I come off the phone with Ashby than Nicola arrived home early from work. She seemed upset.

'What's up?' I asked.

'It's Adam. I just had a call at work from his headmaster. They couldn't get through to the house, the line was engaged.'

'I was on the phone with Chicago. What's wrong?'

'He had an accident. Fell in the playground and knocked himself out.'

'I'll go over right away.'

'No, they've sent him straight to hospital. He's at the Middlesex.'

We took a cab and got to casualty just as Adam was being wheeled in for a brain scan. One of the teachers was there, a woman called Hammond—Olivia or Olga or something, I forget. A red-faced woman in plimsolls with carroty hair and freckles. Good-natured, yet not content in her good nature. She came across to us, flustered.

'Dr Alton, Mrs Alton—there's really nothing to be worried about. Adam's just had a fall, he hit his head, so they've got to check him out, but I'm sure there's been no damage.'

'Is he still unconscious? Mr Willoughby said he was unconscious when the ambulance came.' Nicola was on the edge of panic.

'Yes. Yes, that's right. It was a heavy fall. He seemed to trip, hit his head on the ground.'

'Were you there? Did you see what happened?'

'He was running, he . . . pitched forward suddenly, almost as though he'd been pushed; but there were no other children near him at the time. I think he just caught his foot on something.'

The brain-scan completed, Adam was wheeled out again. We followed him to the room where he was to be kept for observation. I was glad Nicola could not see him, pale and almost lifeless beneath white sheets, or see the wires connecting him to the electroencephalograph next the bed.

Mrs Hammond made herself scarce, full of profuse apologies for the accident, as though it had been her fault. I watched her narrowly as she went, germinating a suspicion that perhaps it really had been.

We were joined a few minutes later by the doctor who had conducted the brain-scan.

'You're the boy's parents? Excellent. My name is Metcalf. I'm a consultant neurologist. They called me down the minute your son arrived. I'm sorry, I didn't get his name.'

'Adam.'

'Adam. Very good. Well, first of all I'd like to reassure you that Adam doesn't appear to be in any immediate danger. I need to study the tomographic scans more closely, of course; but my first impression is that there are no fractions, no swellings, nothing that appears life-threatening. Normally, I wouldn't do a CT scan this early, but he is concussed, and I'd like to keep him under close observation till he wakes up.'

'How long before he wakes up?' Nicola's voice was awash with apprehension.

'Hard to say. You can never quite tell with head injuries. But I'd guess an hour or two. You'll probably have him jabbering away and asking for chocolate the minute he opens his eyes.'

'What about the EEG?' I asked.

He glanced at the instrumentation, as though seeing it for the first time.

'All the readings are within the normal limits. Nevertheless, I'd like to keep him hooked up till I'm fully satisfied it's going to stay that way. Now, if you wouldn't mind, I'd like to ask a few questions about his health in general. The teacher who brought him in wasn't very sure.'

Dr Metcalf's hour or two became a vigil of seven weeks, the longest seven weeks Nicola or I had known. Most of that time Nicola remained by his bedside. She listened to his softly measured breathing, as another mother might have watched his eyes for the first flicker of consciousness. I relieved her when I could get time off work, and in the evenings. There was a clock on the wall facing me. I remember how my eyes would stray towards it, again and again, counting the seconds and the minutes as they dragged themselves past without the slightest sign of recovery on Adam's part.

Dr Metcalf confessed himself worried; but further CT scans showed nothing, the EEG readings remained stubbornly within the limits of normality, all other tests proved negative. Metcalf remained in charge of the case, but colleagues were brought in from time to time, each expressing himself perplexed by Adam's obstinate refusal to surface from the mysterious depths into which he had sunk.

A bed was made available for Nicola so that she could sleep near Adam. She would not leave his side except when she had to, and the staff did all they could to make her comfortable.

I stayed at home alone those nights. Without Adam and Nicola, the house seemed big and empty. I felt a profound depression when I woke each morning, and when I went to bed I would often lie awake for hours just listening. Partly, it was intense worry about Adam. But side by side with that went a growing sense of foreboding. I'd destroyed the photographs I'd had developed in December. I'd thrown away the newspaper cuttings Ed had kept about the plane crash. I'd gone on acting as though nothing was wrong. But something was wrong, and inwardly I knew it.

On the second night I had a nightmare. Perhaps it was not surprising under the circumstances. But I do not think it was brought on by worry. I do not remember much of it, only waking terrified and catching for the light switch beside the bed. Three things I remember: I was in a city so old it did not have a name; there was a full moon that cast a pale light over buildings unlike any I had ever seen before; and at the end of a long tunnel something was waiting for me.

In the moments after I switched on the light I became conscious of a very deep silence all around me. And yet I am sure that, as I woke, just before my fingers reached the switch, I could hear a ringing or jangling sound somewhere in the house, very faint, yet more real than a sound heard in a dream.

Adam remained stubbornly comatose, but without any visible cause. Then, quite abruptly, exactly forty days after the accident, events took a curious turn. Strange patterns began to appear in his

EEG readings. Metcalf, alerted by the duty registrar, said he could make no sense of the printouts. There was marked activity in the delta and theta zones, but other areas of the brain appeared abnormally sluggish. Metcalf ordered another CT scan to be done right away. It too showed abnormalities. Most of the hippocampus and all of the two amygdalas were swollen.

Otherwise, Adam continued as before, unreachable and devoid of vital energy. Seven days later, the abnormal EEG faltered and returned to normal. Five minutes later, Adam opened his eyes for the first time since the accident. Nicola told me later that she almost jumped out of her skin when his voice broke into the silence, hoarsely demanding to know where he was and what she was doing there.

He did not look back from that moment on. Metcalf kept him under observation for another forty-eight hours, during which time he recovered his old spirits completely and developed a roaring appetite that kept him eating almost constantly. All the tests now proved conclusively normal and, with the usual admonitions, he was discharged. A physiotherapist came to the house every day for a week, and in days Adam's somewhat atrophied muscles began to regain their former tone. He started exercising, and his strength returned rapidly. A week after leaving hospital, he was pronounced ready to return to school. Regular check-ups were declared essential, and visits to Dr Metcalf at the hospital's neurology department became a Monday morning ritual.

The night he got home, I asked him if he remembered much about his fall.

'I remember I was running,' he said, clearly having difficulty recalling the event in any but the most hazy detail. 'And then . . . I think I was pushed.'

'Pushed? Who pushed you? Can you remember?'

'It wasn't one of the other children,' he said. 'None of them were anywhere near me.'

'What about Mrs Hammond? Maybe she accidentally . . .'

He shook his head. 'She was where she always sits, on the bench.'

'Why were you running so fast? Can you remember that?'

He frowned.

'I was . . .' He hesitated, and I noticed a flicker of fear in his eyes, as though he was not merely remembering the incident, but reliving it.

'It's all right, Adam. I'm here. Go on.'

'I was being chased,' he said.

'Who was chasing you?'

He caught his breath sharply.

'No one,' he whispered. 'No one.'

It was the first time he ever lied to me.

Chapter Seven

The statue of Shabbatil remained locked in the storeroom at the museum. Adam's emergency drove all thought of it from my head, and pressure of other work meant that I kept putting off a proper examination. After his return, however, I found myself thinking of it more often. I dug out Ed's journal, intending to find out what I could about the background to the discovery and anything he or Caroline had been able to find out in the short time the statue had been in their possession.

The entries started straightforwardly enough. This was not the formal record of the dig—that had been kept by a colleague and taken back to Chicago—but Ed's own private observations, written down every evening between supper and bedtime. Sometimes they did not deal with expedition matters at all, but were personal comments on anything from the state of the food to the latest novel he was reading. There were several following Caroline's death that I found painful in the extreme. Some of them might have seemed the product of a deranged mind, had I not seen and heard what I had. In the end, I decided that it would not serve Ed well to send the journal on to his department. If they ever asked me what had happened to it, I'd say it must have gone missing in the post.

Some of it bears quoting here, if only for the light it sheds on what happened later.

> *15 July*
>
> *That goddammed Mustafa burned the bread again. Not to mention that the stew tasted like mud. He only knows how to cook one damn thing, so why can't he get it right? Why can't we get a proper cook?*
>
> *I'll tell you why! Mustafa's brother Ihsan is a cousin of' somebody called Safi or Samir, who's related to the mayor of Hilla, who has the ear of somebody on*

the provincial council, who married the aunt of a man in Baghdad who has supper every other Thursday with Saddam Husayn. Ergo, Mustafa could keep his job even if he served us the giblets of a five-month-dead dog.

Caroline's name for Mustafa is Gog. Ihsan, who supplies the dead spaniels or whatever they are, is Magog. Gog and Magog. She has names for everybody. Abdul-Ghaffar, the site foreman, is Beelzebub, Lord of the Flies, because he swats anything that comes within two feet of him. Hamid, who's in charge of transport, glories without knowing it in the name of Sindbad the Sailor, because he boasts of having served heroically in the navy during the war against Iran.

There have been more problems with the local workforce here than on any dig I've ever known. Most of them are Shi'ites from Hilla, but I don't think that's the root of the problem. There are a lot of the usual grumbles: low pay, long hours, working outdoors in the heat, not enough equipment to go round, the bus picking them up late, and so on. Nothing to get too wound up about. It wouldn't be an expedition without dark murmurings over the tea.

But there's something else going on here, something I'm at a loss to understand. The men say they don't like working out here. They think we're mad to sleep on the site overnight. At one point I did seriously suggest they make a small camp here themselves, instead of bussing in and out of Hilla every day, but they turned it down flat, even with a promise of extra pay. I know some of them like to spend the night with their wives; but even the young, unmarried men shook their heads and opted for the inconvenience of the bus.

Some of the older men have a curious name for the site. They don't call it 'Babil', which is the proper Arabic term, but 'Bab al-'Uyun', which means something like 'Gate of the Eyes'. Abdul Ghaffar told me it refers to the evil eye. That may be true, but possibly it has another explanation. I'm not much of a linguist, but I'd like to look into it, just to see if there's some sort of folk memory of an older tradition.

17 August

That wretched man Abdul-Ghaffar really is getting on my nerves. First of all, there was yesterday's accident. One of the men lost an eye when a piece of scaffolding came loose and hit him full in the face. Of course, site safety is Abdul-Ghaffar's responsibility, but when I asked him how it happened, he made out he'd inspected the scaffolding in question personally just the day before. I had a look at it myself, and it was obvious the wood had been on the verge of breaking for some time. But no amount of argument, even when backed up by a direct inspection of the scaffolding, made the slightest impact on him or caused him to deviate from his story by so much as a millimetre.

Today, four men have gone missing, leaving us badly undermanned. Abdul-Ghaffar again.

'They see ghost, ya sayyidi, they afraid come back.'

'Ghost? In broad daylight?'

He shrugged in that eloquent manner the southern Iraqis have been practising for generations. He's a marsh Arab, one of the Bani Feraighat clan. He left the marshes thirty-odd years ago, and I often wonder why. Very likely chased out for some crime or other. He makes himself out to be pious, and says he moved north to live near the shrine of Ali at Najaf.

We argued for almost an hour, but I gave up in the end, as I always do. He wouldn't give me the real reason for the men's absence. I just told him to make sure he had four replacements for tomorrow, though we all know that means keeping a close eye on the new arrivals to make sure they know how to do their job properly.

20 August

Caroline thinks there may be some infill near the Ishtar Gate. It came to light by accident more than anything. When that scaffolding fell down, it loosened some of the masonry and made a hell of a mess along a section of wall. Caroline took a little group there this morning, to tidy up as best they could. They decided to dismantle the wall completely before putting it together again. While they were taking some stones away from the western section, the infill was uncovered. We start digging there tomorrow.

21 August
An odd thing happened tonight at supper. Soggy rice and overdone stew as usual. The stew has a different name each night, as though Mustafa was giving us a guided tour through regional cuisine, but it's the same thing each time. We were tucking in with our usual lack of abandon, when one of the Brits, a young guy called Nick Parrish, said something strange.

'You know,' he said, 'I could have sworn I saw old Pete Lazenby down near the Ishtar Gate this afternoon. I was on the point of saying hello, then he went out of sight behind the gate and I lost sight of him. I tried to catch up, but by the time I got there he'd gone. Can't think where he got to. Thought he might have turned up at supper.'

Maurice Price, who just got in from Oxford a few days ago, laughed. He's always in a good humour: he hasn't had enough of Mustafa's cooking yet.

'I hope to God not,' he said. 'The old bugger died last week. Ninety-something and blind as a bat. Funny bloke—never could stand him personally. Too much of an amateur.'

Parrish went extremely pale. I don't know if anybody else noticed it, but I did. A few jokes were made about his getting more sun than was good for him. He passed it all off with some obscene remarks about what other people got up to during the siesta, but when the conversation moved on to other topics I saw him sink back in on himself. I think he still believes he saw Lazenby.

The excavation at the infill is going well. Nothing of any interest yet, but Caroline has an idea the area escaped damage when they were removing material to use as building stones for Hilla back in the twelfth century.

I never met Lazenby myself, but I've heard the usual stories about him from time to time. Not a nice guy by all accounts. But Price was unfair all the same. Lazenby's book on Babylon isn't the work of an amateur. He knew things about this place that nobody else had a clue about.

22 August

I was woken last night by somebody playing a flute. Damnedest thing. Happened about three in the morning. I asked Abdul-Ghaffar if there are any shepherds round here, but he said not.

25 August

Caroline's crew found some skeletons today. There appear to be at least two rooms under the infill. I've looked it over, and I don't think it's a burial site. Not inside the city, and not built the way it is. If we can date the skeletons, perhaps that will shed some light on it. My own suspicion is that we're looking at the medieval period, certainly no later than the foundation of Hilla. There could be any number of explanations for the presence of several bodies in one grave, the most likely being violence of some kind. This isn't far from one of the old caravan routes: was this where a gang of highway robbers hung out?

27 August

More skeletons, and what looks like a statue of some sort. Caroline's very excited, and I don't blame her. Even if the skeletons are medieval, the statue almost certainly isn't. From what we've uncovered of it, it definitely isn't Islamic. Maybe the burials are older than I thought.

28 August

Most of the statue's uncovered now. He's an ugly

bastard, but fascinating. I've seen nothing like him before, nor have any of the others. There's to be a pow-wow tonight, just to see if anyone comes up with theories about his provenance.

Caroline said something odd this morning. We were dressing in our tent at the time.

'Who's the old man?' she asked.

'Old man? What old man?'

'The one I saw yesterday evening near the infill dig.'

'One of the workmen, I suppose.'

'No, they'd already gone home. Anyway, he wasn't in Arab dress.'

'Some sort of official, maybe.'

'I don't think so. I've seen him a couple of times before. Thought he might have been a visitor from Baghdad, maybe even a tourist. He doesn't look Arab. More European or American.'

'Beats me. You know what the tourist board's like. They tell people the site's closed, but you can sneak in and have a look around for a small consideration.'

'Could be.' She finished buttoning her dress. 'But he was all alone, and quite old. And another thing . . . '

'Yes?'

'For a moment last night, I thought he was blind. It was just an impression. He had that way of moving.'

1 September

The English guy, Parrish, had some sort of fit today. Poor bastard, he's in bad shape. His nerves have gone completely, and I think he's headed for some sort of breakdown. Pressure of work or something. That Lazenby business got him down: started thinking he'd been seeing things, wondering if his mind was giving way. Hell of a thing. I like him, he's a nice fellow. Maybe his sex life did for him. He used to make out he was getting laid regularly back in Hilla. Went down there nights. Said there was some sort of temporary marriage joint the Shi'ites used, like a brothel only religious. They call it mut'a. *It's regular enough, but you've got to be a Shi'ite. Parrish isn't even Muslim. But he said he got by. He's that sort of guy. Rick gave him some Valium and told him to spend the day in bed. Let's hope that's all that's needed: he's a key member of the team, and there's no way we could replace him at this point in the season.*

4 September
My darling Caroline died this morning. I don't know what I'm going to do without her. The awful thing is that she died alone. She was sick, and I told her to go to the tent to take a rest. When I came back here at lunchtime, I found her on her bed. I thought she was sleeping at first, then it dawned on me that she wasn't breathing. I just sat and stared at her for maybe half an hour, and all the time I thought I must be going out of my mind.

She'd starting writing me a note, but mustn't have been able to finish it. There were just fourteen words: 'Destroy it now. Destroy everything. The gate must remain closed. He's already watching the . . .' I tore it up. She must have been going into a fever when she wrote it.

That was the last entry. There were no more pages in the journal. Ed —or someone—had torn them out.

Chapter Eight

I am tired now. Years have passed since those events, and in some ways my memory is blurred. Maybe God has pity on me at times. Maybe the mind has its own ways of finding peace. But the central horror never really leaves me. It just subsides for a while before resurfacing when I least expect it to: in the middle of a meal, during a warm bath, at the moment I pass from one room to the other. Or just when I look up from my reading. That's all I have to do. The variations are endless, but the result is always the same: renewed fear, renewed loathing, renewed palpitations. My heart will give out one day soon, fully aware of how it has been deceived.

It's not just memories, of course. The house has more than memories to keep me afraid. Friends tell me I should leave, get myself a smaller place, blot out the past. I wish I could. But the past is always with us, it never dies. And just as you and I wait for morning, so it waits among dreams to reawaken.

Spring and summer passed. Adam was given a clean bill of health by Metcalf, who regarded him as a sort of medical celebrity. He had come through his dark night of the soul unscathed. Or so it seemed. Certainly, no scanning device and no electrodes could pick up any sign of damage. How could they have done? The damage had been caused at a much deeper level. Looking back, I think I understand now why things were quiet for so long, why we thought all had returned to normal when in fact it had not. The thing within Adam was still incubating.

Autumn came like a slap in the face. One day we were in summer, enjoying warm, comfortable days and short, languid nights. The next, we were shivering as a high wind stripped the city of its warmth. The sunshine and the warmth struggled to return for the next few weeks, but all in vain. In the end they gave up the fight, and we put on our coats and jumpers and lit the first fires of the new season.

Adam returned to school after the holidays, strangely eager to be back in the classroom. We'd been to Spain, and he'd enjoyed himself hugely, so I'd rather expected to find him sluggish on his return to the grey streets of London, and reluctant to exchange the brief freedom of the summer for the restrictions of a new school term. Not a bit of it. He was up in the morning ahead of us, bustling with energy, his satchel packed, his sandwiches in their box, his cap and scarf already on, straining at the bit.

On returning from school, he'd go straight to his room and start on his homework. When that was finished—there was never much of it—he'd look for more to occupy himself with. He gave up watching the videos with which he'd previously entertained himself, proclaiming them 'kid's stuff', toddler fodder quite unsuited to his new status as a seven-year-old miracle of modern medicine.

In the mid-term exam he came top of his class by a very wide margin. We were delighted, and enormously relieved by this very tangible evidence that his accident, far from harming his mental faculties, had almost done him positive good. It was only gradually that it dawned on us that, far from good, it had inflicted a terrible evil on him, and that, had he died in hospital, it would have been best for everyone, including Adam himself.

The first hint we had that all was not as it should be came in a phone call from Mrs Hammond, who had become Adam's teacher that year. She rang one day in October, soon after I got back from work. I took the call myself.

'Do you think I could see you and your wife some evening at the school? I'd like to talk about Adam.'

'Has he done something wrong?'

'No, nothing wrong. It's not that sort of problem, not discipline. In a way, it's the opposite of a problem, or so you might suppose. It's just that I think he's working too hard, and I'd like to find out why.'

'I never heard a teacher say that before. None of mine anyway.'

She laughed, then seemed to sober.

'To tell you the truth, Dr Alton, I've never had a pupil like Adam in all the years I've been teaching. He finishes projects before the others have barely started. Gets to the end of one book and wants to run on to the next. He's not skipping lines or missing out pages—I ask him questions about what he's just read, and he gets them right.

He's already started reading books more suitable for eight- or nine-year-olds. Surely you've noticed.'

'Not really. He just takes what he wants from my library here at home. It's got a lot of my old schoolbooks and storybooks. I'm not a teacher, it's hard for me to work out what age-range any particular book is for.'

Nicola and I popped in to the school a couple of days later. The conversation repeated itself for Nicola's sake, then we were shown examples of Adam's work side by side with that of other pupils. It began to sink in that we were standing on the edge of some sort of abyss.

'I don't want to be premature,' went on Mrs Hammond, her little protruding eyes popping yet further from her skull, 'after all he's still only seven; but I think we may be facing a prodigy situation. It could become a problem."

'Problem?' Nicola sounded indignant. 'Surely . . .'

Mrs Hammond shook her head.

'Things that seem like blessings can often turn out problematic. Prodigies don't tend to grow up into happy children. They lose touch with their peers, they end up spending more time with adults than is good for them, they often become bitter and frustrated people. A child's emotions with an adult's brain. That can be hard to live with. And hard to cope with for everybody around them.'

'There were never any signs of this before,' said Nicola. The woman's worries were setting her on edge. 'It's very early days yet. He'll calm down.'

But he did not calm down. As the autumn progressed, so the speed of Adam's uptake accelerated. One evening, picking up my copy of *The Times*, I noticed that someone had been doing the crossword. A good half or more of it had been filled in, and I knew Nicola could not have done it. Double-checking, I found that every solution was correct. When asked, Adam admitted that he had been responsible, but said he'd been unable to complete the whole grid. Later, looking through the remaining clues, I wasn't surprised that he'd been stymied: so was I.

'Did your mother help you?'

He shook his head.

'You worked them out for yourself?'

He shrugged. There was something furtive about his manner.

'It's not hard once you work out how it's done. Some of them are really easy. It's just tricks with words.'

'How long have you been doing crosswords?'

He shuffled uncomfortably, as though afraid of giving something away.

'A few weeks,' he said. 'Off and on.'

I began to suspect that he was fooling them in school, that his reading age had already progressed far beyond that of an eight- or nine-year-old. I'd tackled my first *Times* crossword at the age of fifteen. It had taken me two weeks and the help of several dictionaries. And another year before I could get all the solutions.

It was not just Adam's intellectual attainments that moved forward with unnatural speed. In the space of a term, he experienced a spurt of physical growth that must have put two inches on his height. He outgrew his shoes. His school-cap, bought at the beginning of the academic year, would no longer fit his head.

That term he made firm friends with another boy from his class, Simon Passmore. Little Simon was Adam's foil and counter-image. Physically, they looked unalike. Where Adam was dark-skinned and black-haired, with deep-set smouldering eyes, Simon was pale and fair, and his blue eyes gazed innocently out at the world, naked of duplicity or suspicion or anger.

Simon started coming to our house regularly after school. I remember him well, but from a distance of time that blurs his features in unsettling ways. He was a bright child, yet retiring. Nicola's blindness frightened him at first. He'd stay for a late tea sometimes, and I'd notice him watch her cautiously as she poured tea or sliced bread, his eyes fixed on her slender hands, almost willing her to scald herself or run the serrated edge of the breadknife across a careless finger. Thinking back, of course, I realize he wasn't willing it at all, quite the contrary. Simon had an innate compassion, he was frightened for her, yet his shyness held him back from saying so.

The two boys would spend hours together in Adam's room. They'd play computer games, or Adam would help Simon with his homework. It was always that way round. At other times, I'd hear them talking earnestly together, though I could never quite catch what they said.

Then, one day in November, passing Adam's door when I knew they were both inside, I heard their voices as usual. Suddenly, there was a third voice, a man's voice. I went back and opened the door. Only Adam and Simon were there, my son on the edge of the bed, Simon at the desk, drawing.

'I thought I heard voices,' I said, rather lamely.

Adam looked at me. He eyed me quite coldly, I thought.

'Simon and I were talking.'

'I thought I heard another voice as well. Did you have a tape or a CD-Rom playing?'

Adam shook his head. The computer was switched off. Simon looked at me, and I thought he seemed worried.

I left, still hearing the man's voice in my ears. And there was something else, something I could not identify at first. It only came to me when I was back downstairs again. A familiar smell, one I had smelt there before: a perfume of oriental spices. It had been hanging on the air of the room as I entered, as though brushed there by the lightest of hands. Or as if someone carrying spices had just been walking through.

Chapter Nine

Simon Passmore's pathetically shrunken body was found about three days before Christmas, in a shallow grave covered by a pile of dead leaves in a wood not far from Sevenoaks. He'd gone missing two weeks earlier, in the course of a school nature study trip. There were no marks on his body. A post mortem examination showed no internal injuries or poisonous substances. All that could be determined was that the boy's heart had stopped suddenly, possibly within a day of the trip. Just how long he had remained alive after his disappearance, and what had happened to him during that time, were complete mysteries.

It was a mystery too how he had come to be in the woods, miles from anywhere the school party had actually visited. And who had dug his grave and buried him in it, then covered him with that rug of leaves?

There was another odd thing, though I knew nothing of it until much later, when I happened to hear an account of how Simon's body was discovered. I was listening to the radio one Sunday afternoon, not really listening very attentively, when a programme came on about child murders and their impact on everyone involved, from parents to police. Halfway through, Simon's death was mentioned, and the interviewer spoke to the woman who'd found his body.

Her name was Marjorie Vere-White, a woman of impeccable diction and strong opinions who had been in the woods walking her dogs, something she did every day, though seldom in that sector. I pictured her in a headscarf, clearing the undergrowth in her path with sweeping blows of a stout stick, shouting at the top of her voice at the weaving figures of two spirited retrievers as they dashed about among the trees. 'Folly's the bitch. Got a good nose, scents at a distance, wind or no wind. Tell a hare from a rabbit in a force ten gale. She was the one to get the scent first. Not the boy, that wasn't what she noticed. I thought at first it was the leaves. She was pulling me that way, you see, dragging on the leash and straining hard, and I was tugging her back. "Come on, you stupid dog," I kept saying, "there's nothing there but some old leaves."

'I hadn't been thinking about the missing boy, though I'd heard something about him on the radio. Bad business that, children going missing. Too much of it. Well, Folly just kept on pulling. She's a powerful dog, so I just gave her her head and slipped the leash. Made straight for the leaves. "Stupid animal," I remember thinking. "Won't find a thing in there."

'Next thing, there she was scrabbling about in the leaves mad as a hatter, and when I caught up I made to grab her collar. Wanted to get the leash back on. Damned dog turned her snout and snarled at me. Never knew her to do anything like that before. Not that sort of dog.

'Well, that's when I noticed it. Hadn't been the leaf-smell that brought Folly over. Not a bit of it. There was quite another smell there. It had gone later, after they dug him out of the grave.'

'You recognised it, did you? You knew it was a body?'

'Body? No, wasn't that. Boy hadn't started smelling. Well, maybe he had, I didn't notice. He was under the ground, y'see. No, it was another smell, a funny smell, what I'd call spicy. It was everywhere. All round the grave. Didn't know it was a grave then, of course. Not till Folly started digging.'

'Where did this smell come from, this spicy smell?'

'Where'd it come from? No idea. But it was very strong that day. Reminded me of Egypt in the old days. Used to get smells like that in the souk. Not what you'd expect outside Sevenoaks.'

I visited the grave some time after that, just to see for myself. There was nothing left of the grave itself, of course; not by then. Grass had grown over it again, and it was hard to make out the lines of the scar left by the digging. But someone had been there a week or two before, Simon's mother or father perhaps, and left cut flowers above the spot where he'd been found. It seemed strange to me at first: they had a proper grave, I thought, where he'd been laid to rest in a fitting manner, with prayers and sobbing, and a dull snow falling from a dull sky. But when I reflected, I understood what grief could bring. He'd been in that untended place two weeks alone, without a coffin, in the bare earth. Perhaps they thought more of that unconsecrated burial than of the other. Perhaps they went there more often, how would I know?

From the moment of Simon's disappearance, something changed in Adam. I put it down to shock at first, but it was not that. I am sure he knew his friend was dead all along, and it would not surprise me to learn that he understood perfectly what had happened.

On the evening of his return from the school trip, he locked himself in his bedroom. Nicola and I were a little concerned, but we thought he just needed to be alone for a while, that he had to find his own way to come to terms with the loss of his friend.

I went up about midnight to see if he was all right. The door had already been unlocked, and Adam was in bed, reading.

'Do you need anything?' I asked. 'You haven't eaten since you got home.'

'I'm all right.' Swamped by bedclothes, he seemed small and vulnerable.

'Would it help to talk?'

'Talk?'

'You know. About Simon. About what may have happened to him. Sometimes we worry about things before we know what's really going on, we let things get blown out of proportion.'

'I'm not doing that. I've not been worrying about Simon. I've been working.'

His eyes strayed to the desk. I looked across at it. Its surface was covered in stacks of paper. He must have gone through several pads in a single evening.

'Do you mind if I take a look?'

I saw him hesitate for a split second, then he smiled and nodded.

He'd been working his way through the Concise Oxford Dictionary, and had already finished writing out a considerable section of the letter 'A', words in one column, definitions in the next.

'Why are you doing this?' I asked.

'To learn English properly,' he said.

'But you're learning English at school. You can't just go through a dictionary. Most of these words are too old for you.'

He shook his head.

'Not now I know them,' he said. He smiled again. At least, a smile touched his face. I wondered what was going on behind those eyes.

'Try me,' he said. 'Ask me the meaning of any word.'

I picked up a sheet of paper.

'What does "abecedarian" mean?'

'It means something arranged in the order of the alphabet. Like your dictionary.'

I tried several more entries on him. Each time he answered, not by rote memory, but in his own words. He had assimilated the meanings, worked out what things really were, what linked one thing to another.

I closed the book and looked at him. He was staring at me as if he wanted to see inside my head, to guess what I was thinking. I found myself ducking mentally. And something unsettling occurred to me. He had said he wanted to learn English properly. Not like an English child of seven, but like a foreigner who has come to attend classes at a language school.

I put down the sheet I was holding. As I did so, I noticed some papers underneath the others. These had not been written on, but drawn on by a child. They were oddly reassuring after the adult-like work taken from the dictionary. I lifted one up.

'This is good,' I said, trying to make out what it represented.

'It isn't mine,' said Adam. 'It belongs to Simon.'

I remembered seeing Simon at the desk, bent intently over his drawings.

'Are they all his?'

'Yes.'

Adam seemed uneasy that I was looking at his friend's work. Was it because he feared Simon was dead? Or was it something else?

I picked up a few more of the sheets. Simon had been working in black crayon, pressing hard into the paper, so that small lumps adhered to its surface. There was a similarity between the drawings, as if each represented an attempt to draw closer to an ideal image. I did not know what order to place them in, but still I could make out some sort of progression. It was at the fifth or sixth that the seemingly meaningless scribbles began to take on a more coherent shape. And then, turning the last sheet by forty-five degrees, I saw quite clearly what Simon had been trying to draw. It was the statue I had taken to the museum, the statue he had never set eyes on, the image of the god Shabbatil.

Chapter Ten

I remember the funeral, the snow all morning, falling but not lying, birds circling above the cemetery, men in black coats, women with black armbands, the graves stretching into a distance that would not come into focus. I whispered everything to Nicola, describing the scene to her in perfect detail, the small coffin above all. She'd liked Simon, their brief acquaintance had endeared him to her, and she'd taken his death badly, as though he had been closer to her than a mere friend of her son. When we made love that night, she cried out as though something had been lost to her for ever.

All of Adam's class attended the funeral, and several of the teachers, but it was thought too distressing for the children to be present at the graveside. They were in the church for the service, and together they sang a hymn. There was something pretty and moving about it, and something ugly, as though an unnamed fear had slipped through its cage and entered our reality. Our children, dressed for what might have been Simon's eighth birthday party, singing the praises of a God without pity, little adults suddenly, come to bury their friend.

With Nicola at my side, I watched Simon's parents covertly, from a little distance. We had not met them before, though we'd spoken on the phone to one another from time to time that term. That half-friendship made it more difficult for us to cope with their grief.

After the burial, we returned to the church to pick up Adam. We found him deep in conversation with another boy near the font.

'Mum, Dad—this is Michael. Michael's Irish, from a place called Dublin. He's in my class. I've asked him back to look at my new CD-Rom.'

'I don't think that's a good idea, love, not today.' Nicola bent down to stroke Adam's cheek, but he pulled back. It was the first time I had ever seen him do that, for he knew better than anyone how important physical contact was to his mother.

'I'm sorry, Michael,' I said. 'We'd love to have you over, but we're all a bit upset after the funeral. Maybe Adam can bring you round another day soon.'

At that moment, Michael's parents came up, intending to take him home. They introduced themselves. Their name was Brennan, they were sorry not to have spoken before. Wasn't it tragic to be at the burial of one so young? She was young, and had clearly found the funeral a strain. He was a doctor, a paediatrician working at the homoeopathic hospital in Great Ormond Street. I watched them go, their son between them, his hands held tightly in theirs. Every child had departed like that, hand in loving hand, like a treasure threatened by highwaymen.

We were woken that night at about 3.00 a.m. Nicola came awake first. Her hearing was far more sensitive than mine, she could be roused from sleep by the softest of sounds if it was out of the ordinary. Moments later, I too came up from a lake of sleep, like a drowning man rising to air, and for several moments I lay in the darkness, bewildered. I was not sure if Nicola had woken me, or something else.

'What is it?' I began. I didn't have to ask whether anything was wrong. I could feel it in the atmosphere. Something was very wrong.

'Shhhh.'

I fell silent, and a moment later I heard it consciously for the first time, the tinkling of a small, tinny bell. I tried to remember where and when I had heard it before. It was not a burglar alarm in the distance, not the telephone, not the doorbell—nothing like any of those. Just a light, fragile tinkling that shot through the cold air quickly and vanished, like the little bell they ring in churches during Mass. Several moments of silence followed, then it came again.

'It's inside the house,' said Nicola. Not for a moment did I doubt her. She could pinpoint the direction from which any sound had come with uncanny accuracy. As far as I knew, there was nothing in the house that might have made such a sound. No ornaments, none of Adam's toys, none of the kitchen gadgets. And I remembered at last that I'd woken from sleep while Adam was in hospital, just to catch a brief tinkling that I'd dismissed as part of a dream. What I heard now was no dream.

'It must be Adam,' I said. 'He must have brought some sort of bell home from the funeral. Maybe one of the other boys gave it to him.'

I switched on the light, blinking hard to stop my eyes stinging. Beside me, Nicola shook her head. She was sitting bolt upright, her head craning forward.

'No, ' she said. Her voice was hushed, and I sensed her fear. 'It's not coming from his room.'

'Where is it?'

She shook her head again.

'I'm not sure. It moves each time. As though somebody's walking through the house with it.'

The bell jangled again, leaving the imprint of its presence on the cold air.

'Could it be Adam? Could he be sleepwalking? He's been acting so strangely lately.'

She shook her head.

'I don't think so.' She hesitated, on the verge of saying something important. 'Tom, do you remember, about a year ago, I told you I thought there was something in this house, a harmful presence?'

'Yes,' I whispered. 'Yes, I remember.'

'I've kept quiet about it since then. I thought it might lessen, that the sense of it might fade away. And for a while it did. Then it came back. It's done that several times: faded and returned, faded and returned.'

She paused again, turning her face to me.

'It's come back again, Tom, stronger than before. It's out there now. Walking through the house.'

'What? And making a tinkly sound like Tinkerbell?' I almost laughed out loud. I thank God now that I did not. 'I'm going out to see what it is,' I continued. 'If it is Adam, he either needs help or a stern word about ringing bells in the middle of the night and waking people up.'

I pulled aside the bedclothes and made to clamber out, but Nicola grabbed me hard by the wrist.

'No, Tom, please. For God's sake, don't go out. Let it go past. It won't last much longer, I'm sure of it.'

'You seem to know a lot about it. For something you haven't seen.'

I bit the words back as soon as I uttered them. They'd been thoughtless. There was a great deal Nicola had not seen, but which she knew a lot about. Such as myself.

'It's blind,' she said. 'Blind and . . . something else. I'm not sure what, I don't understand. It's not from this place, but I think it's been here a long time. In this house.'

'How can you know this?'

'I sense it.'

There was a flesh-creeping jangle as the bell sounded suddenly loud outside our door. I held my breath tightly, as though whatever was out there might be leaning with its ear against the door, listening for signs of life within. If it had ears, if it was capable of listening. As I lay there thinking all this, I became uncomfortably aware of something else—a faint smell that seemed to have drifted in under the door. A smell of eastern spices.

I looked hurriedly at the bedside lamp, then remembered what Nicola had said, that it was blind. There was no point my asking how she knew: she just knew. The bell jangled again, still near our door, then a soft footstep padded away across the landing and down the stairs to the next floor. The sound of the bell faded slowly, passing farther and farther from our room.

'It's at Adam's room now,' whispered Nicola.

I jumped out of bed. This time Nicola did not try to stop me. As quietly as possible, I made my way to the door and opened it. Light from the room flooded the landing: everything seemed calm and normal. Suddenly, the bell sounded from below. I felt a hand touch my arm as Nicola came up behind me.

We started to go down the stairs. As we did so, I glanced round to see that Nicola was all right, and my eye caught something I had not noticed before. On the wall, at about shoulder height, a long, uneven line tracked its way across the wallpaper, running from our door all the way down the staircase. I reached out my hand and touched it. It was wet and slightly sticky, and dark purple in colour. It almost resembled blood, but I knew it was not blood. I pictured the blind thing making its way down the stairs, one arm held against the wall to steady and guide itself.

There was a short passage off the next landing, on which Adam's room was situated. It was in total darkness, but as I reached it, I became aware of two things: the smell of spices, stronger than ever, and rough breathing. In spite of Nicola's assurance that the thing could not see, I had a deep reluctance to switch on a light. Perhaps it was less fear that we might be seen than revulsion at what I might see.

A car went by outside, its hissing wheels tearing the silence of the night to shreds. A dog barked on the other side of the street. Beside me, Nicola shivered in the cold. I put my arm round her and pulled her close. Now we had come down here, what were we to do?

I switched on the light. Its sudden brilliance dazzled me, and I blinked hard. When I looked again, I saw for just a moment something dark crouching at Adam's door. The next instant, it was gone, and all I could see was the door itself, gaping open. I ran to it and looked inside. The room was empty. Adam had disappeared.

Chapter Eleven

The next few hours were hell. I shall not forget them. There are moments in the middle of winter when all seems lost, and the darkness presses in and presses in like death, and everything is cold, and I wake in the night shivering, and relive all I went through then. Nicola was rigid with fear all the rest of that night. We were not alone, of course. A policewoman stayed with us until after nine o'clock.

They found him shortly before that. He was alive, but cold and very confused. A gardener had found him wandering in Highgate Cemetery, dressed only in pyjamas and slippers. The police took him to Queen Mary's Hospital, where he was kept under observation until that evening. They were allowed to speak with him, but he could tell them nothing of substance. He remembered getting ready for bed, being tucked in by Nicola and myself, and then finding himself alone in the cemetery around dawn. From the state of his feet, he must have walked across the heath to get there. He himself had no memory of that. But it was reasonably obvious why he had gone.

He was found not far from Simon Passmore's newly-filled grave, and his hands and knees had clay on them, as though he'd been scrabbling there. The grave itself had been badly disturbed: wreaths and bouquets had been thrown aside, a large hole had been dug in the clay, and the small temporary cross bearing Simon's name had gone.

The gardener who found him told us that Adam had at first answered him in a language other than English.

'It were a funny language. Don't reckon as I've 'eard it spoken in these parts before.'

I wondered if Adam might not have unconsciously picked up a little Arabic from his father before he left. But later, when I tried some out on him, he made no response.

He was discharged from the hospital at eight o'clock, and we took him straight home, all three of us silent in the car while I drove through a light mist. The night before, something had come for Adam and had led him to the cemetery. What I wanted to know was why. And whether it would come again.

That night the house was quiet, though I think none of us slept very well. We moved Adam to the guest room, next to our own bedroom, and it was agreed that he should sleep there every night until we were reassured that there would be no more unsettling visits. Nicola would have been happy for him to sleep with us, but I resisted the suggestion, pointing out that he might find it very hard to sleep on his own again. She acquiesced, but reluctantly. I did not know then what she had seen, of course. She had more reason to be afraid than I. And, yes, I did write 'seen'. I'll explain when I'm ready.

The following day, Adam went to school as usual. That too was part of getting things back to normal as quickly as possible. He seemed to have suffered absolutely no harm from his adventure, and we were eager to play down what had happened. He returned from school that afternoon accompanied by Michael, the Irish boy. They went straight to Adam's room and spent a couple of hours together, talking intensely, as children often do. Nicola told me about it when I got home. She'd been a bit upset at first by how casually this new child had replaced Simon in Adam's affections.

'I wouldn't worry about it,' I said. 'They change friends easily at that age. I'd rather he was spending time with this Michael than sitting up there on his own, brooding.'

'What happened the night before last, Tom?'

I hesitated. I'd thought of little else since then. All I knew for certain was that Nicola and I had heard a bell tinkling, and that Adam had gone missing, had gone walking across the heath as far as the cemetery. And beyond that I knew nothing, really. The sound of the bell might very well have been produced by Adam, perhaps already walking in his sleep. Nicola's fears about a blind entity walking the stairs and corridors of our house might have been no more than fancy. How could I know what went on in the mind of a blind woman, shut off for so long from visual contact with the real world?

'Nothing,' I said. 'Really, nothing. Adam was disturbed by Simon's death. He knew his way to the grave and he managed to get there under his own steam.'

'And the sound? The bell?'

'There was no bell. We imagined it.'

'Both of us?'

'We got carried away. There may have been a bell somewhere, I don't know; but . . .'

'I don't imagine things, Tom. There was a bell. Wait. It will come again.'

Michael came almost every day after that. A couple of times he stayed until mid-evening. I met him then, and found myself much taken by him. He was not soft like Simon, but pugnacious and lively. I thought he would be good for Adam. He seemed less brooding, less given to introspection, and Nicola and I agreed that he might do much to bring Adam out of himself. All the same, we were a little worried to see how much Michael seemed in awe of Adam, and as much under his spell as Simon had been.

We visited Michael's parents in their pretty Child's Hill apartment. A sort of solidarity had developed among the parents of children from Simon's class, and we felt it appropriate to get to know the mother and father of Adam's new best friend.

Seán Brennan had been a keen musician in his student days, and the walls were covered with photographs of serious-looking men playing a variety of instruments, bodhráns and uilleann pipes and whistles. On the mantelpiece stood a line of silver cups, trophies of competitions across the length and breadth of Ireland. He himself was a comfortable-looking man of about forty, not fat exactly, but far from lean.

For all our efforts on both sides, it was a stilted evening. He talked about medicine entertainingly enough, painting for us the differences between his practice in Ireland and that in London. But he had no interest in other topics, in books or plays or films, and archaeology provoked little more than polite interest. His wife, whom I remember best for her darting, discontented eyes, remained almost entirely silent throughout the evening, and there would be long gaps in the conversation, barely filled by Nicola and myself.

Her name was, if I remember correctly, Maeve. She came from a family that traced its descent to the High Kings, and in her manner was something of the hauteur I associated with pure blooded Arabs I had met in Baghdad, *sayyids* of holy lineage, descendants of the

Prophet. I knew nothing of Irish snobbery, indeed I'd thought there could be little of it since the Anglo-Irish left or were tamed, and I found her slightly condescending manner disconcerting. But perhaps it was not condescension, perhaps she was just wary of my own presumptions.

She was a religious woman, but out of tune with the church she attended. I imagined her, a pale child at some convent school in County Limerick, coming out to a world that was not quite shaped to her demands.

Only once in the course of that evening did she grow animated.

'Michael is doing very well at school since he started to be friends with Adam. Their teacher says they're now number one and number two.'

'You must be pleased,' said Nicola politely. We'd hoped to avoid offspring comparing, that bane of every parent's life. 'Where was Michael before that?'

'Oh, not so high, you know. Number ten or eleven, quite far down. Your son's a good influence. He works hard, he sets Michael a good example.'

I thought of Adam's own sudden spurt in intellectual precocity. He'd been about mid-way in his previous class too. Who or what had been his example? I'd caught sight of a book on his desk before we went out that evening. The babysitter had noticed it too. It had been Peter Lazenby's *Babylonian Religion and Its Antecedents*. He'd taken it from the library. I'd said nothing.

A week later, Nicola missed her period. A visit to our doctor brought rapid confirmation of her pregnancy, and a calculation in bed that night made it clear that our expected child had been conceived on the night of Simon Passmore's funeral.

Chapter Twelve

Extract from Nicola Alton's Braille Journal:

5 December

The baby inside me is growing too fast. Adam wasn't like this, not in the least. I know they say each baby is different, that one shouldn't make comparisons, but I'm not talking about little quirks and idiosyncracies. This baby is rushing to be born. I almost think he could be born in weeks rather than months.

6 December

I had my first midwife visit today. She did the usual checks, though she took longer over everything than my previous woman. Her name is Margaret Dempsey, and her hands smell of lavender. I didn't tell her my feelings about the baby, she wouldn't understand. I'm in tune with my body, being blind has done that to me, but other people think I'm fancying things. Tom has started to think that too. Not about the baby, but about the things I heard, the things I sense as though I see them. Sight is not all in the eyes, nor hearing in the ears.

7 December

The midwife asked me to come in today in order to meet my obstetrician and to have an ultrasound scan. I'm only six weeks pregnant, and it's unusual to do a scan before sixteen weeks. She says they wanted to check the growth of the foetus, that the results of some of my tests had been puzzling.

Dr Hamilton is the obstetrician. He's a Scot from Dundee, rather bluff, but kind. I think he'll do, but he's a bit old-fashioned. He disapproves of natural births, home births, water births—anything that seems to undermine his own authority. I'm not sure if that's what I want this time, but I'm told it's hard to find anything more enlightened in this area. I may ask little Michael's father if he knows of a better way. They don't do births at the homoeopathic hospital, but I've heard they attend births, and I think they have trained midwives. There are groups of midwives who will do the whole job without a doctor, except where there's an actual emergency. Maybe that's what I need.

Hamilton found the scan puzzling. He said it was 'interesting'. That was his word. I asked what he meant. I couldn't see it, of course.

'Oh, nothing,' he said. 'Nothing for you to worry your pretty head about.'

I could have punched him.

'That sounds as though I should worry.'

'No, not a bit of it. The bairn's fine. Well, it's no a bairn yet, of course, but it is making excellent progress. Rapid progress, in fact. Much more developed than I'd normally expect at six weeks. It looks more like ten. I think there may have been a slip-up at your GP's. You're further on than you thought, Mrs Alton.'

8 December

I hold my hand over my stomach and imagine I can sense the baby growing inside. It's a boy, I don't need a scan to tell me that. He floats inside me with big eyes open wide, growing like a mushroom in the darkness.

Khalil once told me that his people had special prayers for the growth of a new child in the womb. Some of the women could more or less control the baby's growth, as though they could exercise conscious control over the process of gestation.

I have no such control. The baby grows as it wants to grow, and no thought or wish on my part could make it speed up or slow down.

9 December

I remember the night the baby was conceived. Hamilton is wrong about the date, but he wouldn't believe me if I told him. It was the night of the day we buried young Simon Passmore. A cold day, with a wind that reminded me of Scotland. It was cold in bed at first, then it grew warm, and Tom touched me so gently I found myself ready to make love, even though my thoughts were elsewhere, dwelling on that sad little grave with its wooden cross. Tom was more urgent than usual, and he roused me as I've seldom been roused. I don't know quite what happened. One moment, I was distracted, responding to him almost mechanically, my thoughts on Simon's grave, then I remember thinking of Khalil, and the first few times we ever made love, and a spasm went right through me, and I held Tom tight to me and rolled on top of him, and then I thought of the American, Ed, and then of the statue he brought here. I couldn't get the statue out of my head, and the more I thought of it the stronger my physical need grew, and I put Tom inside me and rode on top of him until I came, and I do not remember ever coming like that before. Tom came at the same moment. That was when the baby started. The statue has something to do with it, I think.

24 December

Adam is less excited about Christmas this year than last. He's too much of a little adult now to admit to the unrestrained enthusiasm he used to show, and he says he no longer believes in Santa Claus. That had to come, I suppose. His present list this year was very strange: books, mostly, and some computer software neither Tom nor I had ever heard of. I've bought Tom a pair of expensive shoes. They won't last long, he wears them into the ground.

Mum and Dad arrived this morning. Dad's well, in spite of his turn earlier in the year. Mum seems a little more strained than usual. They're both delighted about the baby. Mum said she thought I looked a little peaky and gave me a whole list of vitamins and supplements that she says I absolutely must take twenty times a day. When I was pregnant with Adam, it was all anxiety about how I'd cope. She'd have rather I'd handed him over for adoption. It's not just a generational thing. I've lost track of the number of people my own age who say I can't be a fit mother.

Tom's mother hasn't come up this year. The weather in Devon has been dreadful, and her roof was badly damaged in a storm. She daren't leave the house unoccupied till it's been properly repaired. It's a pity. I'd been looking forward to being with her again. I never had a chance to meet Tom's father. He died seven years ago. It's a pity—from what Tom tells me, he was an interesting man. A master at a small public school, and an amateur musician. He used to play the shawm with an ancient music consort. He could do the *Times* crossword in ten minutes, and cook perfect risotto, and dance the Foxtrot. Tom's mother misses him dreadfully. I can hear it in her voice every time she speaks of him.

Adam and I had a strange conversation this evening. We'd been sitting round the fire, roasting chestnuts and swopping stories about what we'd all been up to this year. During a lull in the conversation, my mother asked Adam what he was hoping Father Christmas would bring him. She hasn't yet caught up with the fact that he's given up listening for the sound of sleigh-bells jingling through the night air.

'I don't know,' he said. 'I haven't thought.'

'Haven't thought?' She sounded genuinely shocked, as though he'd uttered an obscenity. 'You must be the only boy your age in the whole world who hasn't thought about what he'd like for Christmas.'

Tom told me later that Adam looked at her almost wearily. 'I'm not so sure about that,' he said. 'They don't have Christmas everywhere. There's a girl in school who doesn't have Christmas. She's a Hindu.'

I felt impelled to intervene, to prevent the misunderstanding I could see developing between them escalating any further. But my mother rushed on.

'Oh, dear, how unfortunate for the poor child. She's missing out on so much. It's such a lovely time of year. The carols, the crib, the three wise men, the baby Jesus in his manger.'

We were in for it then. Mother, enchanted by her own memories of happy childhood Christmases, waxed eloquent on kings, angels, frankincense, myrrh, shepherds, and moving stars.

She believes it all, every word of it, and I long ago gave up arguing with her about it.

When she finished, I expected Adam to pump her with questions. He has not had an orthodox upbringing in any sense. He knows that his father was not a Christian, and I think he identifies a little with the possibility of an exotic heritage. But he simply listened without a murmur, then said it was time for bed. He kissed his grandparents and Tom goodnight, and I took him upstairs.

While I was tucking him into bed, he caught hold of my wrist and asked, 'Do you believe all that? All that Christmas stuff, angels and everything.'

'Not really,' I said. 'Not the way your grandmother does. I don't expect you to either.'

'But what about Jesus? Do you believe that?'

'I wish I did,' I said. 'It would make life easier.'

'Easier?' He wriggled down into the warmth of the bedclothes, his feet paddling the hot water bottle I always made for him. 'Why would it make life easier?'

'Darling, you're much too young to understand. A lot of people my age find it helps them if they believe they'll go to heaven after they die.'

'Is that what you think will happen to you?'

I shook my head, remembering how, when I was his age, my mother had promised me heaven and Jesus and an eternity of light. How wrong she had been, how quickly the darkness had reached out for me. Sometimes the darkness became so hideous, I would have sold my soul for light. The devil is not called Lucifer for nothing.

'I think that when we die we go back to where we were before we were born. It's not a place, I think, but a condition. Like a very long sleep.'

'Is that where Simon is now?'

'As far as anyone knows, I'd say yes. I wish I had better answers for you, darling.'

'And is that where I'll go?'

Our chat was growing morbid. I didn't like the turn it had taken, the seriousness with which Adam pursued the matter.

'Not for a very long time, and maybe not at all, dear. None of us really knows what happens when we die. Now, let's switch off your light. You never know, maybe there is a Santa Claus, and maybe he will land on our roof.'

I switched the lamp off and kissed him. His forehead was very cool.

At the door, I said goodnight. Adam's voice crossed the room to me.

'Simon isn't sleeping,' he said.

'Why do you say that, love?'

'Because it's true. He's still on earth. He can't find anywhere else to go. He's lost.'

'How do you know this, darling?'

'He speaks to me.'

'How does he do that?'

'When I'm asleep.'

I crossed to the bed again and bent down, kissing him.

'It's good that you still think of Simon,' I said, 'but you shouldn't let him prey on your mind. Think of something else tonight. And have good dreams.'

25 December

A strange thing happened while we were

unwrapping our presents this morning. We'd opened almost everything: Tom's shoes—a pair of Church's, very fine, if I may say so—and a most beautiful set of tape-recordings of the entire works of Shakespeare, which he'd bought for me. And silk ties and Liberty scarves and delicate perfume and bath oils. I embarrassed everyone by accidentally unwrapping some lingerie Tom had chosen for me. It's very sexy, but I don't know how long I'll be able to wear it if baby goes on growing at this rate.

The bulk of the presents were for Adam. He did have his books and computer software, but his grandparents had brought or sent items they obviously thought more suitable for a boy of his age: games, magic tricks, a small cricket bat, some Lego. He played with them politely after lunch, but his mind wasn't on them and he quickly lost interest.

Among the parcels bearing his name under the tree was one wrapped in plain gold paper and tied with a blue velvet ribbon. Tom said it stood out from the rest, more by its simplicity than anything. Adam opened it to reveal a small box some three inches by four, a blue velvet box with his name embossed on the lid. There can be no question that what lay inside had been intended for him. He lifted the lid to show, nestling on a bed of blue silk cloth, a small object of terracotta. Tom described it in detail to me later. It was about three and a half inches long and two wide, shaped in the form of a small man. The face had been painted in gold, flaking in parts. It was clearly very old. Tom identified it as Babylonian.

Adam lifted it from the box to examine it, while the rest of us looked on (or, in my case, listened) with tightened breath.

'Who could have sent such a strange thing?' my mother asked. 'Isn't there a note of some kind, maybe a name on the label?'

The label was scrutinized again, to no avail. Tom scrabbled among the loose papers and strands of ribbon around the tree, and later he and my father made a thorough search of the room, but they found no note of any description, no clue whatever as to the identity of the gift's donor. It remained equally mysterious how the box had got there. No one had seen it before that moment.

As he raised the figure to examine it more closely, Adam noticed something that had escaped even Tom's expert attention.

'It's a whistle of some sort,' he said. 'Look, there's a mouthpiece here at the feet, and the mouth is open.'

He must have lifted it to his lips. For no perceptible reason, I felt my heart go cold, and stretched out my hand to touch him, to stop him. It was as if I knew that, whatever he did, he must not blow the whistle.

But even as my hand touched his, he had put the little instrument to his lips and blown three short notes on it. My heart clenched like a naked fist to hear it. I can still hear it in my head, not high and shrill as might have been expected, but quite low, almost flute-like. As if it was calling, summoning, wakening . . .

26 December

I think I know now what Adam summoned yesterday. We all went to bed about midnight, the mystery of the unsigned parcel still unsolved and still on our tongues. To accommodate my parents more easily, Adam slept with them in our bedroom, while Tom and I stayed in Adam's room, which has a double bed. I fell asleep almost at once, the sound of the little whistle still ringing in my ears, and just beyond it, almost out of my range of hearing, what seemed to be a man's voice, whispering.

I don't know if I had dreams. But I do remember waking. When I first went blind, that was the hardest part, for I would be dreaming in full daylight, my eyes open, seeing everything, and then I would wake and open my eyes and there would be nothing but darkness. It took me years to learn to cope with that, and even now there are times when it unnerves me.

When I woke last night, I knew instinctively that I was fully awake. But I was not in total darkness. The room was dimly lit by traces of moonlight falling through the half-open blind. Tom was still asleep beside me. I did not waken him. Though I had never seen the room before, I knew its contours very well by touch, and I had no doubt that what stood in front of my eyes was Adam's bedroom. I opened my mouth, almost crying out in the certainty that I could see. I knew it was not a dream.

Suddenly as I blinked my eyes, I caught sight of something moving near the door. I looked directly at it. It was a little boy of seven or eight, dressed in school uniform. For a second, I thought it must be Adam, then I noticed the boy had blond hair, not dark. He opened his mouth as though to speak to me. He looked frightened and bewildered, and there were tears in his eyes and on his cheeks. His clothes seemed mud-stained, and one sleeve was torn. Just as he was about to speak, the darkness descended and I was left staring into my blindness as ever.

I shook Tom awake and told him what I'd seen.

'Seen?'

'I could see, Tom. For a few seconds. There's moonlight, isn't there?'

'Yes, but . . .'

'And Adam's door is green.'

'Nicola . . .'

I described the little boy. Tom said nothing at first. I thought he would disparage me, but he did not.

'You say he had blond hair?'

'Yes. I don't know about his eyes, they were in shadow.'

'What colour was the uniform?'

'Brown and yellow. A yellow stripe along the edge of the jacket collar.'

'You say his sleeve was torn?'

'Yes. The right sleeve.'

There was a protracted silence. When Tom spoke again, it was in an altered voice.

'Simon,' he said. It was almost a whisper. 'You saw Simon Passmore.'

Chapter Thirteen

*N*icola's Journal continued:

15 January

The baby does not stay quiet. They are worried about it at the hospital. They say nothing, but I sense them looking at one another in the middle of silences, exchanging meaningful glances. Dr Hamilton tries to reassure me in that soft, paternalistic voice of his. 'The bairn's coming along fine,' he says. 'You're very advanced, and maybe the pregnancy's going faster than it should, but the bairn himself is alive and well.'

I don't understand how this ultrasound business works. They've all described it to me, and what they see on their screen; but without something to touch, I can't really picture it. I imagine it's a bit like a photograph, so that's what I take it as. I don't think it can show them what's really there.

17 January

I was at home on my own all day today. Tom was at work, Adam was at school, and I had a day off. I've been getting somebody at the university to record some journal articles onto tape for me. I don't want Tom to know about them. Something is going on that requires explanation, and I want to get to the bottom of it. Sense says I should speak to Tom about it directly, but he's so guarded recently, and I don't want to put him more on the defensive.

When we first arrived here, I used to love being in the house alone. It felt safe and friendly, I got to know my way around it without a moment's unease. In my thoughts, I used to picture it filled with light.

Now, I stay in my study and think about what may be on the other side of the door. Old houses have their presences, but this one has more than its share. The floorboards creak, the joists shift, the rafters settle, and I listen to it all intently like a child who hears the blood pounding in his head for the first time, and thinks it is bears in the attic.

I'm not listening for the floorboards or the joists, of course. They're perfectly natural, they don't frighten me in the least. Just an old house shifting in its sleep. What I listen for is not natural. Footsteps. The ringing of a tiny bell.

I can't stay in my study all the time, of course. I have to use the bathroom, or find clothes in the bedroom, or tidy Adam's room, and that means going upstairs. The staircase is very quiet always. I walk up slowly, as I used to do when I was newly blind, a step at a time, unconsciously counting them. I pause on the half landing and on the landing of the floor above, and I brace myself for the next climb. For all I know, they are all around me, watching. They know I can't see them, and if they stay very quiet, I can't hear them either. They won't let me touch them, they know better than that. By the time I get back to the study again, my heart is pounding, and it takes me twenty minutes or more to calm down again.

I'm not sure who they are, but I know they are there. I've said nothing about them to Tom, he wouldn't understand. I've only been aware of them myself in the past few weeks. Is it because of the baby, does it make me more aware? We'll see.

Something happened while I was still alone this afternoon, around three o'clock. That's when I usually get ready to pick Adam up from school, on the days when I'm not at work. He and I walk home together. It's a bit silly, I suppose, because I'd not be much use in fighting off child molesters or muggers. He'd probably have to defend me. But it gives me a chance to speak to him properly, before he busies himself in his books upstairs. I envy him that, of course. I used to love reading myself. Braille isn't the same.

I was in the hall putting on my coat and scarf when I heard a voice. It came from the kitchen, a man's voice, and for a moment I thought someone must have broken in. But why would a burglar be talking aloud? Two burglars, even. Then there was a burst of music, and I realized that the radio must have been switched on.

The radio was less frightening than burglars, but the question remained of who had turned it on. I'd never known a radio switch itself on, unless it had a timer. Had someone put an alarm-clock radio there without warning me, and had it gone on suddenly, thinking it was morning? I hesitated for a minute or more, but since the radio went on playing, I decided to go in and turn it off. I couldn't very well go out and leave it on. In any case, the more I listened to it, the more ordinary and innocent it sounded.

As I went through the kitchen door, I felt abruptly cold, then warm again, as though I'd passed through a current of icy air. The radio sits on a ledge on the other side of the room. I crossed to it quickly and made to switch it off. But it was already dead. It was switched off, but playing all the same. I worked the switch back and forth, but doing that had no effect, and I decided the thing must be broken. The only way I could turn it off was to unplug it. I traced the wire to the plug and pulled it out of the socket. The radio went on playing.

It must have gone on playing like that for half a minute or more, while I stood with the plug in my hand, listening to the beating of my heart rapidly growing faster and longer. Then suddenly the music stopped. I let out a long breath and waited. Nothing. The room was as silent as it was every morning when I came down to make breakfast.

Relieved by the silence, I turned and started retracing my steps to the door. It takes five steps exactly. I had scarcely reached the hall when the radio snapped on again. This was past a joke.

'Is someone there?' I asked. There was no answer. 'Tom? Are you there? Are you playing some sort of silly joke? Adam? That isn't you, is it?'

For some reason, the music, which had been belting out enthusiastically only a few moments before, had stopped. The man's voice came again, not speaking this time, but chanting softly in a language unknown to me. Strange words, thick and guttural, oozing from his throat in a deliberate, sing-song intonation, as if he was calling me to prayer, or smothering me in treacle. I did not like his voice, there was something inexplicably loathsome about it, as though it harboured a great evil, as if the words he uttered were poisoned.

Elenu ia kima zu-ubbi iwu-ú li-il lidu-ù anaku kia ashabi ina bi-it di-immati shakhu-urru ri-igmi. . . .

For a little while, I still clung to the notion that this was a recording of some Eastern religious music, from Tibet or Ladakh or somewhere similar. Did the BBC still do that sort of thing? Probably not on Tuesday afternoon on Radio 4.

The voice stopped. I held my breath, willing another voice to come, a presenter telling us what we had just been listening to. But no voice came. I was suspended in a void. There was silence, a very pure silence that drifted on too long. And then, just once, a tiny bell rang out, and a young boy's voice came, again in a language I did not recognize. It lasted one or two minutes, then deep silence filled the room once more. I waited for the bell to ring again, but it did not. I sensed an end.

I don't know how long I stood there like that, just listening. If there had been a footstep, or an intake of breath, or a door gently opening, I should have heard it, but there was nothing. Adam arrived not long after that, accompanied by Michael and his mother.

'I thought it best to bring Adam straight back,' Maeve told me. 'He said you'd been unexpectedly detained, and asked me if I'd bring him home. Well, it's on my way, of course, he knows that.'

Adam and Michael went upstairs at once, scarcely pausing to greet me. I offered Maeve tea. She was about to refuse, then said 'yes' and sat down. I sensed something was amiss. I tried to picture her, but for some reason all that came to mind were drawings of nuns from old school textbooks. I was sure Maeve was like none of them, but I had no images of modern Irish women to help my imagination.

'What are you wearing?' I asked, as I poured tea carefully into her cup. 'It helps me to picture you.'

'Well, it's nothing very special, you know. A white blouse and a tweed skirt, with a little jacket over. Very English.' She paused. 'It must be very hard for you not to see.'

'Yes, it is. But I get by. Would you mind very much if I touched your face?'

'My face?'

'It will help me form an impression.'

'Oh, I see. Of course, if you like.'

She leaned forward, and I put my fingers to her cheeks, softly, as I had learned to do so many years ago. My mother first, then my father, relearning the faces I loved. The moment I touched Maeve, I knew something was wrong. Worry, grief, anguish all tensed the muscles of the face, and I've developed a sensitivity in my fingertips, the way some sighted people can tell another's emotion at a glance. My fingers glided deftly across her mouth, her chin, her cheeks, and as they did so I felt her tremble. Coming to her eyes, I felt my fingers grow wet. I took my hands away briefly, then put them back and wiped her tears away. She sobbed openly then, holding nothing back. She reached for me blindly, and I held her while she cried, not loudly, but bitterly for all that. Gradually, her sobs subsided. She drew back, and I released her, taking one of her hands in mine.

'You can tell me,' I said. 'If you want to. It's all right, you can trust me.' I realized she had no one else to talk to, no one to confide in, no close friends.

She hesitated, taking deep breaths.

'Aren't I an awful silly woman,' she said. 'I feel a great fool coming here and bawling over a cup of tea.'

'It's not foolish to cry. I've done my share.'

'We were a dreadful family, you know. Nine girls, and me the youngest. My mother made fun of us if we cried when we were tiny. She said we had to be tough. And then the nuns . . . Well, they'd not much sentiment about them. You'd think life was all about suffering to listen to them. When I married . . .' Her voice faded, and I sensed she was momentarily lost in thought. 'Well, you know Seán is a doctor. He's seen much greater suffering than mine.'

'Is it Michael you're worried about?' I asked. I don't know why, it could have been a hundred things. But that was what I sensed, and I'd learned to go with my instincts. I heard her catch her breath. Her hand tightened on mine.

'Yes,' she answered. 'Michael. My little boy. Something's happening to him. At first I just thought he was getting to be more confident, coming out of his shell. I'd always thought he had great promise, but he was never really showing it. Now, I'm not so sure.'

'What is it? What's happening?'

'Oh, I don't know. I think it's all too much of a strain for him. He works all the time, he never rests. I tell him he ought to watch the television, I say "Why don't you go outside and play with the other children, why don't you make things with your Lego?" But all he ever does is shake his head, and go to his room, and stay in it for hours on end. Seán's no help at all. He worked very hard to become a doctor, he thinks his son should do the same. I tell him it's unhealthy at Michael's age, but he just shakes his own head and goes back to the hospital to see to his patients.'

'I think Adam's proving a bad influence on Michael. He's become exactly the same. "All work and no play . . ."'

'You're right, there is an influence. Michael's a strong boy, with a will of his own, but he looks up to Adam a lot.'

'I promise I'll speak to Adam about it. Get him to take it easy and to lay off Michael.'

'It's more than just the work, mind. I've been looking in his room, and I don't mind telling you I'm a little disturbed by what I've found. There are drawings everywhere. He hides some of them in books—he doesn't think I'll look in them. They're all of the same thing. It looks like some sort of heathen god, maybe something they've been studying in school. He draws it again and again. I am very frightened by it.'

'Did you . . . Did you ask him what this god is called?'

'Shabbatil. He says it is called Shabbatil. Have you ever heard of such a thing?'

I shook my head and changed the subject. We talked a little longer. I tried to reassure her, but there was something else, something she wasn't telling me. I wondered if she'd been hearing noises, little bells jangling in the night, chanting on the radio, God knows what. I should have asked her, but I was afraid of what she might reply.

As she got up to go, she bent down to pick something up. It was Adam's school jacket, which he'd tossed carelessly over the back of a chair. It had fallen to the floor. He'd been brought up to know better than to leave things lying where I could trip over them. I said I'd have a word with him.

'There's something else here,' she said. 'It must have fallen out of his pocket.'

She handed it to me. It was a lump of something heavy.

'It's clay, I think,' Maeve said.

'I can't imagine what it is. Something they made in school.'

'It's just . . .' Her voice sounded strange. 'It has something drawn on it. That figure, the one I told you about. And words written round it.'

'Words? Can you read them?'

'I think so. "The . . . Son . . . of Shabbatil".'

When Maeve and Michael had gone, I remained sitting in the kitchen with a cup of tea and some cake. I wanted to think. I enjoy fine teas, mostly for their scent. This was an oolong, a dragon noir. It cleared my thoughts. I drained the cup and went upstairs.

'How did you know I'd been delayed?' I asked.

'You're always on time,' he said. 'You're never late.'

'But I might still have been on my way. Why did you ask Maeve to take you home?'

'She was going my way. Michael had to go home today. It's some sort of religious holiday, something Catholics have. I thought if she brought me back, Michael and I could spend half an hour together.'

'How did you know I was still in the house?' I wasn't satisfied with his answers; he was holding something back.

'I knew,' he said. 'You were in the kitchen. You were listening to the radio.'

I felt a deep shiver lick my bones. As though cold from another clime had settled on them.

'I didn't tell you that. You can't possibly have known.'

'You didn't have to tell me. I knew. Please, mother, it's better you don't ask. You'll only upset yourself. We can't have that. You've the baby to think about.'

'I have a son to think about already,' I said. I could feel him slipping away from me. He was seven, and he talked to me like an adult. Without fear, without remorse.

'I'm all right,' he said. 'Really.'

'Who is the son of Shabbatil?' I asked. 'Is it you?'

'No.' He spoke without any falsity in his voice, in matter-of-fact tones another child might have used when asked his age or what day it was.

'The baby, then?'

There was a pause. As though he was reaching a difficult decision. When he spoke, I sensed the caution in his voice, and something else, something very like triumph.

'Yes,' he said. 'That's why you have to take care. He's very precious. Nothing should be allowed to happen to him.'

'Who told you all this?' I asked, afraid of my own son for the first time.

'You wouldn't understand. It's not for you to know such things. You have to carry him and give birth to him, that's all.'

'Adam, darling, what's wrong? Why are you talking to me like this?'

'Please, mother, don't get upset. It could hurt the baby.'

That was when I felt it move for the first time. At ten weeks. Much too early. It moved, and I felt a pain slice through me, as though the baby itself was warning me. I reached out to touch Adam's cheek, but he stepped away from me.

'I have homework to do, mother,' he said. 'I'd like to get on with it.'

I turned and left him. But at the door I paused.

'What if I decide to have an abortion? What then?' I didn't even stop to think whether he knew what an abortion was or not. He knew.

He didn't answer immediately. But he'd heard.

'They won't let you,' he said. 'It's better not even to think of it.'

But I do think of it. It's not too late, you see, not really.

Chapter Fourteen

Nicola's Journal continued:

21 January

I think the baby talks to someone while I'm asleep.
I've no way of knowing for sure, but sometimes when I
wake I remember dreams that frighten me. There are
words in them, some English, some in that other
language.

Last night I dreamed I was blind. Does that make
sense? I had dreams like that when I first lost my sight,
for a year or two. All darkness, you see, and me in it,
just as I am when I'm awake in the daytime, seeing
nothing. Normally, I see in my dreams, the way the
lame run and the deaf hear symphonies; though time
and the failure of memory have created strange
landscapes and even stranger faces.

In the dream, I was in total darkness, but without
any idea of where I was. When I'm awake, I always
know exactly which room I'm in, and which way I'm
facing, and where everything is located. I never venture
into a strange environment alone.

I remember calling out several times. Not Tom's
name, as you might expect, but Khalil's, as though I
wanted him back. It was the only sound I heard at first,
my own voice keening for a husband I no longer loved.
Then I seemed to tire or grow cautious. I stopped
calling, and the sound of a low wind, moaning and
chortling at one and the same time, flooded my ears.

I don't know how long it went on, seconds or hours
—my memory of the dream tells me nothing. But it did
stop in the end, and I had the distinct sensation that

someone was standing directly in front of me, only a foot or two away.

'Khalil?' I asked. 'Is that you?'

A strange voice came out of the darkness. No, not quite strange, it only seemed so at first because I had for some reason expected Khalil's voice. That's odd, because I dream of him very seldom. It was the voice I had heard on the radio, chanting. This time he was speaking English. Good English, faultless English, the sort you hear in Senior Common Rooms and the best clubs. It reeked of exclusiveness. I wondered afresh what the other language was.

'Mrs Alton. You're very welcome. It's time we met properly. But why don't you open your eyes?'

'They are open,' I answered. I felt afraid of him, but I had nowhere to go. 'I can't see. I'm blind, you should know that.'

I don't know why I said that, why I thought he should know anything about me at all, but some instinct whispered that it was the case, that he knew all about me.

'That's absolute nonsense,' he responded, 'and you know it. You can see as well as I can, if only you'd make the effort. All you have to do is open your eyes.'

'I told you already, they are open.'

'Not those eyes. I don't mean those eyes.'

'Where am I?'

Since the dying down of the wind, an oppressive silence had formed around me again. And I smelled something: spices, like the ones in the Pakistani grocer's at the end of our street.

'In his house.'

'His house? I don't understand. Whose house?'

'The House of Shabbatil.'

'And where is that?'

'In Babylon. Where else would it be? Come along, it's time we went a little further. You can't stand there all night.'

He touched me then. I would have expected his hand to be smooth and light, like his voice. But it was not. It was rough and cold, and I'm not sure it was a hand at all.

At any rate, that's when I woke, crying out loud and flailing about in bed. Tom woke beside me and took me in his arms, soothing me. When I slept again, I had no dreams.

25 January

Benjamin arrived today. He's my new guide dog. I get round well enough without one, but with the baby on its way, Tom insisted that I get one, to minimize the risk of falls.

I'm not displeased. The dog makes me feel less independent, but I couldn't help falling for him straight away. He's two years old, very well trained, and extremely affectionate.

When my last guide dog died, I vowed never to have one again. Her name was Annabel, and I adored her. She went with me everywhere between the ages of twenty-five and thirty-one. Somebody killed her, we never found out who. I'd been in bed with a heavy cold, and Annabel hadn't had a proper walk for days. Khalil took her out, and somewhere in the park she broke free and ran off. It wasn't like her. Guide dogs are trained never to run away. But something distracted her or frightened her, and she took to her heels. She didn't come back that night, nor the next day. A dog who could have found her way home blindfolded.

A young man found her two days later, her legs and neck broken. That's why I found the thought of another dog unbearable.

But everything else has changed since then. I'm not married to Khalil, I'm not living in Manchester. Benjamin is just another break with a rotten past.

The baby kicked again today. I don't tell them at the clinic, for fear they'll consider me unbalanced, if they don't already. I've said nothing to Tom about Shabbatil, or what happened to Adam.

26 January

Adam was eight today. 'Happy Birthday' I said when he bounded down the stairs this morning. I only had a grunt in reply, the sort of answer you might expect from a teenager. I don't think he likes being eight. He's at war with himself, a rapidly-expanding brain in the body of a child. Eight is better than seven, of course, but it's still miles too young for Adam, who wants to be twenty this year and forty next.

We gave him a set of toy soldiers, fine ones in Napoleonic uniform. Our budget wouldn't stretch to a battlefield, but I said he could spend his spare time making one. They sell kits, and he could save his pocket money for trees and cannon and so on. He said he'd think about it. Tom told me afterwards that he'd picked through the soldiers with little real interest, then put them back in their box like someone packing unwanted items away before a trip abroad. The phrase took me aback. I imagined Adam on a journey, aboard a ship that was steaming as fast as it could away from the shores of childhood. Six months ago, he'd have killed for a set of soldiers like those.

He took the book I gave him to school. That he did like. It's an introduction to the history of the ancient Middle East by someone called Petronelli. Suitable for sixteen-year-olds.

Since today was a schoolday, and the day of a test to boot, Adam agreed to have his party tomorrow, which is a Saturday. It won't be a big affair, just some friends from school, ourselves, and a magician. When I was Adam's age, I couldn't get enough of magic tricks. Later, before I went blind, I learned to appreciate the particular skill behind card tricks. I'd watch and watch, trying to work out how the best tricks were done, but I could never discover the secret. And once I was blind, I lost all interest. Magic without sight is wooden, like music without hearing, or lovemaking without touch.

Chapter Fifteen

We're still shaken by what happened at the party today. There were eleven children, apart from Adam: seven boys, and four girls in party frocks. At first things went as they always do at these affairs: initial awkwardness giving way to laughter, leading to bouts of boisterousness, culminating in teasing, fights, and tears. I handled it all with my usual tact, which means I shouted a little less than Nicola, and somehow or other things didn't descend into utter chaos as we'd feared.

The food was devoured as if no one had eaten for a year. Parental warnings—'don't make yourself sick', 'don't make a pig of yourself', 'don't stuff yourself so full you can't breathe', 'don't spill food on your new dress'—went unheeded, and a table laden with pop, crisps, jellies, cakes, and God knows what else vanished inside a dozen well-fed yet mysteriously bottomless bellies.

Ali Baba the Magician arrived at the front door just as the last glass of fizzy lemonade was being unceremoniously poured down the front of a screaming girl's dress. Nicky and I were heartily glad of reinforcements. Ali Baba knew the ropes so much better than we, and said this was the ideal time for entertainment. Party games on bursting stomachs were bound to end in tears and vomiting.

Not being able to see, Nicola had little interest in the proceedings. But she sat at the back of the room, trying to visualize to herself the tricks Ali was performing. Children are less demanding than adults in these matters, and the tricks Ali chose to entertain them with were simple, but more than enough to reduce them to open-mouthed silence within minutes.

Ali Baba's an Iranian who has lived in London since the Revolution. He's a funny-looking man with a mane of greying hair, an enormous moustache, the biggest ears I've ever seen, and a prominent nose. He speaks English with a fearful accent, yet absolutely intelligibly. His costume was startling, and he told me it was based on the outfits worn by wandering dervishes in the last century. I had the impression that he was less concerned with amusing the children than with filling them with a sense of wonder and mystery. They listened to him as they would never have listened to a parent or teacher.

'We have many names for magic in my language, *Aqa*,' he said while we were chatting beforehand. '*Rawhani, sehr, simiya, jadu, jadugari* . . . We're a magical people.'

'Not too magical, I hope.'

'*Afsus,* what I perform today will not be real magic, just tricks for the delight of children. My family have been magicians since the days of Rustam and Jamshid, *Aqa.* That was before Islam. When this revolution has run its course, my son shall return and continue our tradition.'

'You're not a Muslim?'

He shrugged.

'*Shayad.* Perhaps. Perhaps I am a Zoroastrian. Does it matter?'

I shook my head.

'Not to me. And not to the kids. Is your name really Ali Baba?'

'You don't think someone can be called such a thing? "Baba" means "Daddy". It's an appropriate name, don't you think, *Jinab*?'

I smiled. He was something between Albert Einstein and Coco the Clown. Except that he was cleverer than the first and funnier than the second.

He started with tricks involving about ten miles of silk handkerchiefs, four rabbits (one white, one black, one grey, and one green), and a cageful of canaries. We'd talked about the show beforehand, and he'd agreed that there should be nothing involving sawing volunteers in half, or decapitating them, or shutting them up in sealed boxes, bound and gagged. We didn't want to frighten the children, or encourage them to try tricks like that out on one another.

For his finale, he asked for a volunteer. Every hand in the room went up, but good old Ali knew the score: you don't neglect the birthday boy. Adam was duly singled out and led up to the little stage on which Ali performed.

Ali had wheeled on an elaborate contraption, a tall box shaped and decorated like a Sultan's palace, complete with ogee windows and a golden dome topped by an enormous crescent. It was straight out of the Arabian Nights. A second palace, this one with a silver dome and a revolving Aladdin's lamp on top, was wheeled on and set down about six feet away from the first.

'Behold,' proclaimed Ali, 'the twin palaces of Nur al-Dunya and Zulmat-i Jahan. In the first there dwells the Caliph of Baghdad, the young and handsome Mutawakkil. And in the second lives the immortal genie Ifreet.

'And now,' he went on, turning to Adam and placing a huge turban of gold cloth on his head, 'the young caliph shall enter his palace.'

Adam duly stepped inside the first structure, which was illuminated from inside. His head came to just beneath the dome, the turban fitting almost perfectly inside it. We could see his silhouette outlined perfectly against the opaque side of the palace, which was made of waxed paper or some such material.

Ali asked Adam to move his arms and legs about, so we could see that it really was him inside the box. He performed a little dance, then stood still again. Ali then produced an oversized lamp similar to the one on top of the second palace.

'And now I shall rub Ifreet's lamp and call on him to transport the young caliph from Baghdad the Abode of Peace to the palace of Zulmat-i Jahan, far, far away in distant Hindustan.'

I watched intently, as puzzled as any of the children as to how Ali was to perform this seemingly impossible feat. No doubt Adam's image would be transferred by mirrors or electricity from box one to box two, while Adam stayed where he was. This wasn't a real stage, there weren't any trapdoors in our floor, and Adam wasn't in Ali Baba's pocket.

The light stayed on in the Caliph's palace, but Adam's silhouette disappeared from its wall. Our eyes turned to the second palace, expecting to see it reappear there. Instead, there appeared another silhouette, about the size of Adam's, but horned, with a tail that writhed about its body like a monstrous snake. One or two of the girls screamed. I caught my breath. Then the silhouette changed, and it was Adam, lifting his arms and legs as before.

The children let out a collective sigh of relief that quickly changed to applause. A moment later, Adam was returned to his own palace, and invited to step out for a round of applause from his astonished friends. The children clapped and cheered, and forgot their momentary terror. But they had not seen what I had seen: when the horned figure appeared in the second palace, Ali Baba's face went as white as any man's face I have seen. Something had happened that was not part of the trick.

He left not long after that. I showed him to the door and helped him carry his gear to the van outside.

'You saw what I saw, didn't you?' I said.

He shook his head.

'I saw nothing, *Aqa*. Shadows are shadows. They shift and change.'

'This was no ordinary shadow. It shouldn't have been there.'

'It was the shadow of the wicked genie Ifreet. What else do you suppose?'

'I have another name for it,' I said. 'Do you?'

He asked for his cheque, and I wrote it out. He was good value. I'd have asked him back for my own birthday in six weeks' time, if only to see what he could do for an adult audience. But something told me he'd find another booking in his diary for that date.

I saw him glance round as he drove off. No longer Albert Einstein, no longer Coco the Clown; just a terrified refugee who has seen a spectre from the past.

I think my biggest mistake was going to the door like that, and helping Ali Baba out. In my prolonged absence, the children had prevailed on Nicola to let them play party games, and someone had suggested the perennial favourite of hide-and-seek. It's a game that always goes down well when children are in other people's houses. There's none of the dusty familiarity of home, none of the predictable hiding-places and predictable guesses as to where the others are.

When I came back, I found Nicola alone in the kitchen with a counting child.

'Two hundred and ten, two hundred and eleven, two hundred and twelve . . .' the thin voice droned on.

'She has to get to three hundred,' whispered Nicola.

I realized there'd been no chance to explain to her what had happened in the course of the palace trick

'Do you think this is wise?' I asked. 'To let them all wander through the house?'

'They'll be all right. It's a wonderful way to keep them quiet for half an hour. They'll hardly get lost.'

'I don't mean that. I mean . . .' My voice trailed away as I grew more aware of the little girl next to me. I took Nicola by the arm and steered her to the other end of the kitchen.

'This house isn't safe,' I said. 'The children could be in great danger.'

'Surely not in broad daylight.'

'I think it can happen at any time of the day. Something came during Ali Baba's performance.' I told her what had happened, about the shadow I had seen cast against the walls of the Zulmat-i Jahan palace.

'Two hundred and ninety-nine. Three hundred! Here I come, ready or not!'

Before I could stop her, the little girl had hared off through the kitchen door, hunting her quarries for all she was worth.

'Her name's Shirley,' Nicola said. 'You've met her mother; that big woman with the hairdo.'

I sat down, suddenly overcome with weariness. It never ceased to amaze me how she could remember the physical details of people she had never seen.

'I think we should talk about what's going on,' I said. 'In this house. With Adam. With you and me. It's time we got to the bottom of it all.'

At that moment, there was a cry of 'Found you!' from the living-room, then the sound of four running feet as Shirley and her unearthed quarry set off in search of the next victim.

'It's the baby, Tom. I don't think it's your baby at all.'

I felt as though I'd been slapped hard across the face. I stared at her, not knowing what to say. She frowned, shaking her head.

'I don't mean what you think, love,' she said. 'I haven't been having an affair. In a way, it's not my baby either.'

'You're carrying it.'

'That's not what I mean.'

Another cry came from the hunting children, this time from somewhere upstairs.

'I think you should explain this. Whose baby do you think it is?'

She took a deep breath and told me everything she'd thought and feared. It made no sense to me. How could a Babylonian god father a child? How did a child like Adam come to know so much about the baby his mother was carrying?

'I'm sure you misunderstood him,' I said. 'He was just being protective. He knows no more about this "Son of Shabbatil" business than you do.'

'Speak to him yourself. Ask him. You can't deny that something strange has been going on in this house.'

'No, I don't deny it. That's why I wanted to talk. I think the house is haunted, but not by something from Babylon.'

'Then what was it you saw just now?'

Another series of cries. Feet running in all directions now. Laughter like caged birds in a frenzy.

I had no answer. An illusion of Ali Baba's? A trick gone strangely amiss?

'Very well,' I said. 'Something has to be done. You say you had a dream . . .'

She started to explain, but her account of the strange man in the darkness was interrupted by pounding feet and high-pitched voices.

'We've found everybody, but we can't find Michael anywhere,' called out Shirley as she came running into the kitchen. The others followed her, some hurtling along as though powered by engines, some a step at a time. I noticed Adam hanging back behind them all, subdued.

'Where have you looked?' I said.

'Everywhere!' said a boy with ginger hair.

'Well, you can't have looked everywhere,' I said, 'or you'd have found him.'

'He could have gone outside,' said another boy, called Alastair.

'No, silly, we all agreed,' Shirley snapped at him. I winced, picturing her with her future husband.

'Adam,' I called. 'Have you any idea where he might be?'

Adam shook his head. His long hair flopped across his forehead, and he swept it back like a teenager.

'He knows the house better than the rest of you,' I said. 'Now why don't we see if we can ferret him out.'

We started at the bottom and worked our way slowly to the top, leaving no room unsearched. There was no sign of him anywhere.

'He didn't go home, did he?' I asked.

No one answered.

Back downstairs, I thought of ringing Michael's parents to check.

Adam's surly manner made me think the two boys might have had a falling out. But I didn't want to worry Maeve needlessly. Small boys have ways of cramming themselves into spots you wouldn't think possible.

'Come on,' I said, 'a prize for the first one to find him.'

I was half way up the stairs when I heard his voice. The others heard it too.

'Help me,' he was calling, very faintly. 'Please help me. I can't get out.'

'Where are you, Michael?' I called. I couldn't work out where his voice was coming from.

'Help me. Please help me.'

'Michael. Try to calm down. If you tell me where you are, I'll get you out straight away.'

When his voice came again, it seemed to be from a different direction. 'It's dark. I want out. Please help me.'

Nicola joined me. With her sensitivity to sounds and their directions, I thought we'd track him down in a couple of minutes. But try as she could, she found it no easier than the rest of us. She went up and down the stairs, and all the time Michael's increasingly frantic entreaties came to us as if from nowhere. She would go into a room, thinking his voice was coming from it, and next moment she would hear him across the hallway or on another floor.

'I'm getting scared,' she said at last, when yet another scouring of the house had failed to locate him. By now the children were genuinely frightened, all except Adam, who seemed unconcerned.

I remember us all standing huddled together at the foot of the stairs, listening to Michael's thin, frightened voice passing through the house. I was on the edge of panic. And then it stopped. Silence. My heart rushed to my throat, I could hardly breathe. Beside me, Nicola was standing rigid, her hands tightly clasped.

Then Michael appeared. He was at the top of the stairs, staring down at us. I felt the breath leave my body in a rush.

'Michael!'

He just stood there, staring, saying nothing. I ran up the stairs two at a time. He hardly seemed to see me. I clasped him.

'It's all right,' I said. 'You're all right.'

He felt limp and empty. I took a deep breath. As I did so I noticed something. Michael's clothes were pervaded with the smell of spices.

Chapter Sixteen

The children quietened down quickly after that. Nicola got them playing charades in the living-room. I took Michael to the kitchen and gave him some squash to drink. He gulped it down greedily and asked for more. The others, seeing him reappear like that, assumed he'd just got stuck somewhere they hadn't been able to find. I knew better. So did he. But I thought it better to say nothing of it. Anyway, he was still too shaken by his experience. I wondered where he had been; and I thought of Nicola's dream, and the dark place in it. There are dark places everywhere, but when the blind cannot see in their sleep, it is the darkest place of all.

The next morning a parcel arrived from Chicago. In it was a slim folder containing several sheets of paper torn from a notebook, and an accompanying slip saying that these had been found in a box belonging to Ed Monelli. They were the missing pages of the journal. The note was from someone called Rick Harrison.

'I think these must have been taken from one of Dr Monelli's notebooks. You said you were holding on to them for your work on the statue. I haven't even bothered to look at them, since they probably won't make much sense without the rest. Hope the research is coming along well. Thanks again for sending the other stuff on.'

I took them to work with me. The idea of going through them at home didn't appeal. They didn't take long to read. After I finished, I was tempted to destroy them, but some sort of academic delicacy held me back. Perhaps the same sort of delicacy that had prompted Ed to hide the sheets in a box after having taken the trouble to tear them from the journal in the first place.

I'll just write down what matters here. Some things it's better I keep back. Delicacy or no delicacy, I have already destroyed them, and I've absolutely no desire to bring them back to mind.

6 September

The authorities down in Hilla say none of us can leave till they've done an autopsy on poor Caroline. They took her back up to a hospital in Baghdad: the one here isn't good enough for dissecting foreign corpses. What are they afraid of? That I'll start shouting 'poison gas!' to the first journalist I stumble across? Claim the water supply's affected? Make a song and dance about life-threatening diseases entering the region, maybe spreading elsewhere? Jesus, all I want to do is take her home in a casket and bury her. We don't have a plot back home, but there's a little cemetery down by the lake where we used to go together on summer evenings. It was a good place, quiet, full of birds. She used to say it would be a good place to be buried.

The atmosphere in the camp is terrible. Nobody knows what to say to me. They can't just pass the time of day. The subject of Caroline is just too distressing, so we stick to work and pretend it's all we want to talk about. Digging has stopped, and most of the native workforce has drifted off. They know we're finished for the season now. The rest of us just sit around in the sun or potter about in our tents, writing up notes or fitting finds together. There's a real danger we'll get badly behind in our schedule. Caroline wouldn't have wanted that, not after such an important discovery.

I had a dreadful moment last night. I woke up in a sweat and found I'd fallen asleep with my light on. When I reached over to switch it off, I caught sight of Caroline sitting up in bed opposite, staring right at me. She looked terrible. Then I blinked or something, and she was gone. I've never been so frightened in my life. It was only a second or two, but her eyes . . .

7 September

There's something very wrong with this place. Late yesterday a goatherd came to the site, accompanied by fifty or sixty animals. They were dirty, unkempt creatures, their fleeces smeared with mud and excrement, covered in a thick layer of dust. The boy—he can't have been more than eight or nine—led them down to the river and set about washing and watering them. The bleating drew me from my tent, and I went down to the river-bank and sat for over an hour, watching him.

The scene was almost Biblical. Abraham would have tended

beasts like that at the same age. The descending sun criss-crossed the water with rays of gold that slowly turned to vermillion. The boy brought water from the river in a leaking canvas bucket, and poured it into hollows all along the bank. His goats drank greedily, as though they'd been weeks in the desert.

Catching sight of me watching him, he came up and asked me for permission to keep his herd at the site till morning. His Arabic was strange, as though he was unaccustomed to speaking the language. He didn't look like a Kurd, though, and in any case he wouldn't have been this far south if he was. All he wore was a simple white garment, neither a thawb nor a dishdasha, but something I've never seen on anyone round here before. I wondered if he might have been a Mandaean, but dismissed the idea as quickly as it came. Surely they all speak Arabic nowadays.

I pointed him to a little pasture not far from the site, and warned him not to let any of his animals stray on to the dig. I asked if he could keep that many goats under control.

'Na'am, ya sayyidi,' he said. 'I can control every one of them. You will see.'

He smiled at me, a very adult smile, and turned back to the river. It was like a river of blood in the dying sun.

Later, sitting in my tent after the evening meal, I heard a pipe playing not very far away, and realized it must be the little goatherd. I stepped out into the moonlight to listen. The air had grown cool, and I shivered, partly from cold, partly from the thoughts circling through my brain. The music seemed familiar; then I remembered the piping I heard a couple of weeks before Caroline's death. I went back inside the tent and broke down for the first time since I found her. Jesus, I can't get over what's happened. I keep expecting her to come through the flap of the tent and sit down over there like nothing's wrong.

I was woken in the middle of the night. I don't know what time it was exactly, but I'd guess well before dawn. I could hear a crazy sound of bleating. Not just the ordinary bleating you'd expect from a large herd of goats. This was something wilder and more frenzied, as if they were frightened by something, a jackal or a large dog perhaps.

I should have got up and gone out to investigate. But my crying bout had worn me out, and I'd taken a couple of pills to knock myself out, so I just turned over and slid back into sleep. The last thing I remember was hearing the bleating fade and the flute music drifting through it.

Somebody woke me about 6.00.

'Ed, you'd better come look at the dig. Hurry up.'

It was Tim Bryant. He was wearing just jeans and sneakers.

'Tim? What happened?' I was still half asleep.

'You'd better come see.'

I pulled on a robe and staggered out. The sun was slanting in from the east, washing everything in a lurid, half-finished light.

'I got up twenty minutes ago,' Tim explained. 'I'd been thinking about that problem with the gate foundations during the night. Thought I'd take a look once there was enough light.'

We came over a little rise and passed through the Ishtar gate. Babylon lay in front of us, red and ochre and jonquil, its stones spilled and tumbled like rocks in a sea of sand. My first thought was that new rocks had grown up there in the middle of the night, grey rocks flecked with henna. Then my eyes adjusted and I saw what had brought Tim headlong to my tent.

For almost as far as I could see, the ground before me was dotted with the bodies of goats. They lay stiffly, with their hoofed legs straight out and their heads back. Their throats had been cut, and everywhere pools of blood lay congealing in the growing warmth. Thick mats of flies had already gathered, and were feasting on the blood. I could hear them buzzing, like a great engine humming away. My empty stomach churned and I turned aside but too late to stop myself being violently sick.

When I looked up again, I noticed someone walking among the slaughtered animals. I thought at first it must be the goatherd, but a second glance told me it was an adult. I couldn't bear to walk among the corpses, so I called out.

'Who's that?'

Whoever it was paid no heed to me. I asked Tim if he recognized him.

'It's Nick Parrish. What the hell's he doing?'

I called his name this time.

'Nick? What are you up to? You can't do anything.'

He looked round and saw us. My eyes were still blurred from sleep, but I could make out his face well enough to see he was in a *state of some agitation. Tim must have seen it too. He walked out to him and brought him back, steering him by the elbow between the bloody carcasses.*

'Nick? Are you all right? How long have you been out here?'

He just looked at me as though I was from Mars or something. Then he started laughing. I've never heard anybody laugh like that before. Christ, I think it scared me more than the goats.

'I'll take him back to the camp,' Tim said, 'give him something to calm him down.'

When they'd gone, I stayed a few minutes longer, just staring at the mess. Great spirals of black flies spun in the sunlight. Every fly within a twenty-mile radius must have been drawn there. And they were still coming. I found myself about to gag again, so I headed back to my tent.

I couldn't face breakfast, but I showered and put some fresh clothes on. I had to think quickly about what to do with the dead goats. If we didn't clear them away soon, we'd have a real health hazard on our hands. I asked Abdul-Ghaffar to see if he could find the goatherd, and he went off muttering God knows what under his breath. He came back about an hour later, saying the boy wasn't to be found anywhere.

'Who could have done a thing like this?' I asked. 'Have you any idea?'

He spat on the ground and snatched his head back in a gesture indicating that he didn't know and didn't care. But I knew the goats were exercising some sort of fascination on him. Fifty to sixty goats represented a lot of dirhams. And, sure enough, he'd already worked it out.

'My cousin Hammad is a butcher,' he said. 'Near Hilla.' He paused. 'If you like, I can speak to him.'

I'd worked it out myself. The best the goatherd could hope for was to earn some cash for the meat. There wasn't any time to lose.

'Tell your cousin he can have a good price if he comes quickly.'

The deal was done, Abdul-Ghaffar got his cut, I took charge of the payment to hold for the boy, and Hammad and his friends cleared the site. Some of the workmen came back from Hilla and spent the' rest of the day removing all traces of the blood. The flies stopped coming after that, but one damned thing still freaks me: I can still hear them buzzing out there.

8 September

There was more piping last night. I went out and woke some of the guys, and we spent over an hour going back and forth, looking for the kid. He wasn't anywhere, but the damned piping just went on and on. We tried again this morning, but the kid still couldn't be found. None of the Arabs claims to know anything about him, but one or two of them looked awkward when I mentioned him. I'll ask around a bit, see if somebody else has heard of him. He can't just have vanished into thin air. Or come from it.

I called in on Parrish today. He's being kept to his tent while arrangements are made to ship him back to England. The poor guy's really ill. I didn't ask him what he was doing walking about among the goats; I'm not even sure he could give me a straight answer.

One thing disturbed me, though. As I was leaving, he called me back.

'Ed,' he said, 'do you think I'm going mad?'

'No, but I think you're ill. You need help. They can handle this a lot better back in England.'

'I've let you down.'

'The work you did here was great. Honestly. I want you back on the team next season.'

'It's just . . .'

'Don't worry about it.'

'I thought I saw Caroline yesterday. Good God, Ed, I know that sounds a dreadful thing to say, but it's true.'

I didn't mock him.

'Where do you think you saw her?'

He hesitated. His hand was shaking, and I thought he was about to lose his grip again. I took his hand and held it steady. He looked straight at me.

'Out there,' he said. His voice was just a whisper. 'With the goats. I was going to speak to her when you called me.'

9 September

Parrish left this morning. Tim drove to Baghdad with him. He'll put him on the plane there. It's a straight flight back to London, and his parents will meet him at the airport. They've made arrangements for him to go into hospital. I think he'll recover once he's away from this place.

The autopsy report came through this morning. It says Caroline died from an embolism. I don't believe it, but what can I do? I need official confirmation of the cause of death before I can take her home. And now the baladiyya *in Hilla says there has to be an inquest. I just want it over with. She's not at rest, she won't be at rest until she's been taken away from here and buried. I saw her again last night, just like before. Next to the chamber where we found the statue. With the boy.*

The piping went on all night and didn't stop till dawn. I can't sleep for it, it gets inside my dreams. When I first heard it, I thought it was a pretty sound, but now I'm not so sure. There's something ugly about it, something unspeakable.

10 September

The inquest was held this morning at the baladiyya. *Most of us went into town, leaving a handful of Arabs at the site. The proceedings were held in Arabic, and I couldn't follow them very well. For some reason, they took testimony from Abdul-Ghaffar and Mustafa. I'm not sure what they said, but there was something about 'the eyes of the city' that caused a flutter in the room. 'Uyun al-madina was the phrase. It reminds me of the name the older men have for the place: Bab al-'Uyun.*

Everything went off smoothly in the end. The autopsy report was presented as official confirmation of the cause of death, and accepted by the coroner. Now it's a case of waiting for stamps and seals. A lot of money will have to pass hands. But I've got the consul in Baghdad involved now, and I plan to get Caroline out by the end of the week.

11 September

After the inquest yesterday I realized that we've been wasting a hell of a lot of time just . . . well, I suppose, just mourning for Caroline. Somehow, getting that all over with helped put us back on track. I had Abdul-Ghaffar recruit a few men before leaving town, and we took them back out to the site. I decided I wanted the chamber Caroline had been excavating finished before I leave. I wanted to be sure there weren't any more finds at that level, but if there were I considered them hers by right, and I wanted them found in her name.

It took five or six hours to remove what was left of the infill. I kept the men working in relays by lamplight. There were no more statues, nothing but minor finds that had strayed into the chamber. But when the rubble was removed from the rear wall, I was called inside.

Abdul-Ghaffar held up a light for me to see by. It cast a harsh white glow across the mud-brick wall, throwing shadows in confusion everywhere. I felt giddy. The atmosphere inside the little chamber was hot and stuffy. There was a faint smell of spices. Every breath I took clung to my throat, drying and tickling it. My head felt light, and my eyes would scarcely focus. In the distance, the call to the evening prayer drifted across the fields. It seemed to go on forever, as though all the calls to prayer I had heard had joined together in a seamless fabric that led back to the very first, and beyond that again to the prayers that had sounded here before Islam.

Allahu akbar, allahu akbar . . .

I looked at the wall. The mud brick had been incised with line after line of identical figures: small eyes, identical to the eyes on the statue of Shabbatil, hundreds upon hundreds of them. I ran my hand along them, tracing the lines as though they held my destiny. I heard a buzzing sound in my ears, like flies.

Ashhadu an la ilaha illa 'llah....

'Look, sayyidi . . .' Abdul-Ghaffar held something out to me. 'This was buried next to wall.'

I looked at him, at what he was holding. My head was spinning. The sound of buzzing was growing louder every moment. I reached out my hand and took it from him. It was a small flute, an ancient wooden flute clogged with sand. I shook it clear and lifted the mouth to my lips. Abdul-Ghaffar tried to stop me, but he seemed insubstantial, like a ghost. I put the flute to my mouth and blew. A single, deafening note filled the chamber. And the flies came in, a cloud of them, and their buzzing seemed to merge with the piping of the flute, and the throbbing chant of the adhan. The last thing I remember is the wall of eyes spinning out of control in front of me.

12 September

Dear God what have I done? Mustafa came to me this morning and told me that seventeen people have already died in Hilla. They think it is on account of the goat's meat sold by Abdul-Ghaffar's cousin. It is tainted in some way. Another forty-seven people are ill.

'*How was the meat tainted?' I asked. 'Wasn't it put straight into the deep freeze?'*

He looked at me sternly, his black eyes burning in his face like small fires.

'*It is the* lahm Iblis,' *he said. 'It is enough.' And he walked out without another word.*

The lahm Iblis: *the Devil's meat. The words will not leave me. The god we found has another name, Baalzebub, the Lord of the Flies.*

Chapter Seventeen

*N*icola's *Journal continued:*

29 January

Tom read Ed Monelli's journal to me last night, all he had of it, from beginning to end, including the pages Ed had ripped out. I was angry that I hadn't been told about this before. What I don't understand is why Ed brought the statue here. Not just to London, but to our house. He must have known he was bringing something evil. Maybe it just didn't matter to him. Or maybe . . . I don't like to think of the alternative.

30 January

My first long walk with Benjie this morning. Through the heath and back. The weather was gorgeous. The air was mild, and in places I could feel the sun on my skin. I must have been stupid not to have a dog all these years.

I went to work in the afternoon and got home just after five. Adam and Michael were already there, up in Adam's room. I've arranged with Maeve to bring them here on days when I have to work. It allows her to get out of the house, and she and I have a chance to drink tea together and talk.

All she knows about Michael's experience at the birthday party is that he got trapped when playing hide-and-seek. I don't intend to tell her anything else, and it's obvious that Michael isn't saying anything either.

She talked more about herself, her privileged but empty childhood, her lack of a proper education, her marriage that was more or less arranged. Seán is kind, but they have no real rapport. His real love is medicine, and she and Michael come quite far down his list of priorities.

I think she finds it easy to talk to me. Being blind makes me almost anonymous, a bit like a priest in a confessional. Her own priest isn't much help, she says. He's very conservative, and counsels her to obedience and other wifely virtues, as he calls them. She's a conscientious church-goer and very devout, but the fact that she has only one child doesn't go down well.

'I've told him that Seán and I don't use contraception,' she told me, 'but he won't believe me. I say it's the will of God, and he accuses me of being wilful and disobedient. I can't talk to him, not the way I can talk to you.'

She has started to tell me about her dreams. Recently, she has been having nightmares. A dark place, she says, and a wall covered with eyes that stare at her without blinking.

31 January

I've been doing a lot of thinking about the baby. It's growing faster than ever now. I've started missing appointments at the medical centre, because I'm frightened of what they may tell me. Dr Hamilton rang this morning. He means well, but he doesn't understand. I asked him about an abortion. There was a shocked silence for about half a minute, then a very stern Scottish voice telling me there were no medical or social reasons that he knew of for terminating the pregnancy. I was tempted to tell him who—what—the baby is.

I'll have to do it myself.

1 February

There was something in the house last night. Tom was away. He had to go to a seminar in Manchester, and I stayed with Adam. I wanted Adam to sleep with me, but he refused, saying he wasn't a kid any more.

'Are you sure you'll be all right?' I asked.

'Don't be silly, Mummy,' he said. 'I sleep on my own every night. Why should tonight be any different?'

Why indeed?

I brought Benjie's basket up to the bedroom. If my son wouldn't keep me company, my dog would. It made me feel much more comfortable, having Benjie there. I'm coming to depend on him more and more. He was a bit bewildered at first by the move, but once I lay down he settled, and I was sent to sleep by his snoring.

I woke just after three. My fingers reached instinctively for my braille watch as they always do, but even as I did so I knew something was wrong. Benjie was growling, a low nervous growl that made my scalp tingle.

'Benjie? Benjie, what's wrong?'

I got out of bed and reached for him, but he wasn't in his basket. I followed the sound of his growling and found him backed against the wall, his fur on end, his teeth bared. When I tried to touch him, he snapped at me.

'Benjie, it's me. It's all right.' I went on talking to him, trying to soothe him, all the time wishing Tom could be with me.

Suddenly, the growling turned to a frightened whimper. Benjie backed further against the wall, no longer aggressive, but terrified. I heard the door of the room open. There's a hinge that needs to be oiled, and I couldn't mistake the sound of it protesting as it always does.

'Who's there?' I held on to Benjie, seeking a protection my rational mind knew he could not offer. 'Is that you, Adam?'

There was no answer, but I knew very well there was someone there. It was cold. My skin puckered against the night air. A little bell rang out somewhere. And suddenly, just like that other night, I could see clearly. The light on the landing had been left on.

Two little boys stood in the doorway. One was

Simon Passmore. I recognized the mud-stained and torn clothes, the blond hair, the outright expression of fear. The other boy must have been Adam: he fitted my son's description in every way, and he was wearing pyjamas identical, as far as I could tell, to those Adam had been wearing when he went to bed that night.

Adam opened his mouth and started speaking. Not in English, but in that other language, the language I was sure by now must be Babylonian.

'Adam!' I cried out. 'It's me. Speak to me properly. I can't understand you.'

Just then Benjie let out a terrible howl. I looked round. There seemed to be nothing wrong. He began whimpering and shaking. I held him more tightly. In the doorway, Adam continued to speak in a sing-song voice, his tones imitating those of the man on the radio. I looked up at him. Behind him, the landing had grown dark. Something like a shadow was moving slowly across the floor behind him. I let out an involuntary cry. Then everything grew dark.

I am awake again. Tom arrived home an hour ago. Adam is at school, though I don't know how he got there. I feel all right, but Tom says I should rest. I'd like to rest, but if I so much as doze off, terrible images come into my brain.

Simon is with me. I think he's been here all along. He just sits and watches. I think he should leave, but he has nowhere to go. He smiled at me last night. I have never been so frightened by anything.

Chapter Eighteen

Nicola's sleeping now. No need to disturb her. We'll talk when she wakes, but only if she's up to it. I'm deeply worried about the effect all this is having on her, and on the baby. I'd like to get her out of here, but it just isn't possible. Houses in London aren't selling, and this one needs too much done to it even to make it worth putting on the market. No, moving isn't an option. We've got to stick it out and get to the bottom of the problem.

I didn't go to Manchester yesterday, but for the moment I'd rather Nicola thought I did. A couple of days ago I had a long chat with Terry Forbes, the colleague who got us this house and who has the unenviable task of cataloguing Peter Lazenby's papers.

Naturally, I said nothing to him about my real interest in Lazenby, nor did I mention the things that have happened in the house that once belonged to the old man. In the short time I've known Terry, I've found him level-headed, sensible, reliable, and remarkably lacking in imagination. A good colleague, but a hopeless friend, and absolutely the last person in whom to confide that one's house is being haunted by God knows what, and that a dead man somehow contrived to have a statue brought halfway across the world for a purpose I had yet to fathom.

'I've made a start on the cataloguing,' he said, filing his fingernails down with the gentle motions of a manicurist. 'But every time I get stuck in, something else comes up and I have to leave off. I'm afraid you'll find it a bit of a mess.'

I looked at the boxes in their cupboard. He wasn't exaggerating.

'Didn't Lazenby at least . . .?'

'God, no. The man was brilliant, but he left everything in a crazy state. He never threw anything away. That's more than half my problem. One minute you're going through a box of personal letters, then you stick your hand in and come up with ten years' worth of bills for the daily paper. It's like a bran tub. You won't find it easy to get hold of whatever it is you're looking for. I take it you do know what you're after?'

'It's just a hunch. I think he had notes on his Babylon work that could answer a few questions.'

'Sooner you than me.'

'Did you know him well?'

'Not really. I don't think anybody did. He kept to himself a lot after he went blind. Even before that, people tended to keep their distance.'

'Why was that?'

He laughed. I watched his long fingers play with the nail file. Clean, well-groomed fingers, without ragged edges or chewed corners. He looked like a man without worries. No wonder the chaos of Peter Lazenby's life repelled him.

'Well, old Lazenby had a bit of a reputation. Something of a ladies' man, I'm told.'

'Why would that make people keep away? Sensible women, certainly; but a reputation like that would hardly make a man a pariah. Unless it was little girls.'

Nick shrugged.

'I'm not really sure. There may have been little girls. Or big girls at least. I have heard he was very good-looking in his younger days. This is going back—oh, just before the last war. Seducing women wasn't quite so simple back then. And Lazenby's thing was undergraduates. That must have been quick tricky: they used to keep them locked up pretty tight. Padlocks on doors, chastity belts for all I know. By the time it got easier, he'd started losing his looks. Not that that stopped him. He had a name, he was very persuasive. But after a while . . .'

He paused and laid the file down carefully on top of his desk. I glanced along it. Everything in its place, pens and pencils arranged in rows, a container for paperclips, another for rubber bands, another for computer discs; no photographs, no evidence of a personal life.

'There was talk of something unsavoury, I'm not sure what.'

'Orgies?'

'No, more private than that. One at a time. I've heard he was into some peculiar religious practices. Maybe the sex was part of that. Who knows, you may find the answer in those boxes.'

I said I'd let him know if anything turned up. He seemed anxious for scandal, like someone whose life craves what it cannot provide for itself.

I took a carload of the brown cardboard boxes home. They fitted almost exactly into the little cupboard beneath the stairs. I remember fitting the last one in, noticing how snugly they all nestled together, like little birds happy to be back home.

I'd made enquiries about Nick Parrish, the English archaeologist who'd left Baghdad like someone who'd stayed too long in a war zone. He wasn't teaching at Cambridge any longer, but Alice Bird, an old friend who'd recently taken a fellowship at Pembroke, told me he'd been taken to hospital the day after he got back from Iraq.

'Can I see him?' I asked.

'I'm not sure. He's out of hospital now, but his girlfriend keeps a close watch on him. He's not allowed many visitors.'

'I'll come down anyway.'

'You can have a college guest-room. We can eat in Hall if you like.'

I said I'd get an early train from King's Cross and meet at Pembroke. Alice would do what she could to get me in to see Parrish.

That evening, Terry called.

'Tom, I've been asking around about old Lazenby. Andrew Hutchins used to go over there a lot. They'd a mutual interest in some Arab poet, they may have been working on a translation, I don't know. Anyway, over the years Lazenby loosened up a lot, told Andrew some things he never mentioned to anybody else. We're talking about reminiscences, of course. By this time Lazenby was blind and pretty well house-bound.

'It started with sex. He was frank about that. No inhibitions. Said he liked women, enjoyed sleeping with them. But he had a hang-up. He would only sleep with virgins. Back whenever, finding them wasn't the problem so much as persuading them that he was worth losing it for. Later on, when his undergraduates were more liberated, the problem was sorting out the virgins from the herd—not an easy task.

'But by that time he was getting the sex mixed up with other things.'

Living with Nicola has made me sensitive to sounds and voices. I notice things most when on the telephone. Terry was revelling in the salacious detail of what he'd leaned, yet his tidy mind was tut-tutting away like a little grandmother sitting inside his skull.

'Everybody gets sex mixed up with something. What was Lazenby into?'

'Religion. He thought the ancient Babylonians knew the truth of existence, knew things that were lost later on. Lost or destroyed. Not just the usual guff about wisdom. He talked about it a lot with Andrew. Look, why don't you ring him up and ask him about it? He knows far more than I do.'

'Hello?'

'Is that Andrew? This is Tom Alton. I've just been speaking with Terry Forbes. About Peter Lazenby.'

'Terry said you were asking.'

I'd only met Andrew Hutchins two or three times, at committee meetings. He was in his late forties, a vain man with a balding head round which a halo of greying hair was trimmed back close to the scalp.

'He says you used to go over there.'

'That's right. I hear you own the house now.'

'In a way. Sometimes I think it owns us.'

He took that as banter, the sort of thing people say about their mortgages. I meant it differently. Very differently.

'How can I help you?'

'I need to know about Lazenby.'

There was a protracted silence at the other end. When he spoke again, I detected something defensive in it.

'This is not cheap curiosity. You wouldn't ring me at home just to gossip about a dead friend.'

'I'm interested in him, I want to know what he was researching.'

'No, it isn't that. It's the house. Come on, man. You can be honest with me. I went there often enough. I spent whole evenings with Lazenby.'

'You went there at night?'

'Always. It amused him. The house would be dark, you see. He'd let me have a lamp or two to see by, otherwise the darkness put us on a similar footing.'

'You know the house well?'

'Well enough. I take it you're having trouble?'

'Yes.'

'If I'd known you were buying it, I'd have warned you off it. It's a bad house, always been bad. You have children?'

'One boy. And my wife's expecting.'

There was another silence.

'Are you at home now?'

'Yes.'

'May I come over?'

We shook hands on the doorstep, and I let him in, standing to one side to give him passage, as one might let a priest in for the last rites, or a doctor, or an undertaker. He stood a while in the hallway, looking round him, taking his bearings.

'You've changed it quite a bit,' he said.

'Not that much,' I said. 'Most of the house is as it was, barring the furniture.'

'You've kept the study?'

I nodded.

'Good, let's go there. And bring some whiskey like a good chap. Nothing fancy.'

'I don't have anything fancy.'

'And bring two glasses. I don't like to drink alone.'

Nicola was typing up her journal, Adam was in his room doing homework. I said I had work to go over with a colleague.

The study was chilly. I lit the gas fire, an old-fashioned one that had been put in by Lazenby God knows how many years earlier. Hutchins looked at it with a grimace of nostalgia, then turned and took the bottle from the table where I had set it.

'A noggin for me,' he said, 'and a noggin for you.'

'I'm not really a whiskey . . .'

'I insist.'

He was behaving like the host. I said nothing and took the proferred glass from his hand. We sat down facing one another.

'I told Forbes about the sex, because that's the sort of thing he likes. I'm not entirely sure what turns him on, but he does like to indulge in tales about the cavortings of his fellow men. For all I know he's never cavorted in his life. On the other hand . . .'

He raised the glass to his lips and took a long, appreciative sip, then glanced at the label.

'Not altogether bad. Now, what have you seen? Or heard.'

I found it hard to talk about it all at first; but slowly, aided by the warmth of the whiskey in my stomach and the gentle fluttering of the fire, I told him all I could. The bell, the whistle, Simon Passmore mud-spattered and dead. He sat and listened like an attentive priest or an old friend, and if I looked up I would catch sight of his bright eyes, focussed, not on me, but on the room; and I detected fear in them, and curiosity, and pity.

'It was never a good house,' he said when I came to an end. 'Even before Lazenby set foot in it. I think that's what drew him to it. He told me there'd been a murder here, sometime back in the last century. There was a large family living here before he moved in: the daughter went mad and was confined in one of the upstairs rooms for several years. He knew all about it, about everyone who'd ever lived here.'

'I think what we've seen and heard here has more to do with Lazenby himself than previous owners.'

'Yes, you could be right. Strange things went on here while he was still alive.'

'Such as?'

Well, there was the sex business, of course. We made light of it at first, but later on it got a bit out of hand. There was something of a scandal back in the early seventies, a couple of years before Lazenby retired. He was banned from all contact with undergraduates after it. I'd just been taken on at the museum, so I only ever heard about it at second- and third-hand. It was all hushed up, naturally. They did that rather better then than now. Some of it leaked out, though.'

He paused and poured a fresh whiskey into his empty glass. The light of my desk lamp caught the liquid as it ran from the bottle neck, sending a spiral of amber gleams through the crystal.

'I'll have more too,' I said, and held out my glass, the first time in my life I'd ever taken a second shot of spirits. He poured a generous measure, smiled, and returned the bottle to the table.

'I met one of the women involved a few years later,' he said. 'It was quite by chance. She was in her first or second year at the time, reading history. When I met her she was working in a post office in Clerkenwell. Never took her degree. Too traumatized by what happened. She hinted at things, but I could never persuade her to go into details.'

'Lazenby raped her?'

He shook his head.

'No, nothing like that, at least in the sense I think you mean. Peter never used force on a woman. He'd have considered it infra dig and a slur on his sexual charms. He wanted them warm and willing. No, by the time this happened, he'd started using his religious ideas to persuade women that having sex with him was the route to physical pleasure and eternal bliss all in one.'

'Terry said something about that. He said Lazenby was after wisdom or something.'

He denied the notion with an emphatic shake of his head.

'Wisdom? Good Lord, no. Peter Lazenby thought he had that in abundance already. What he wanted was to become a god.'

Chapter Nineteen

I took an early train to Cambridge the following morning. Mist lay on the winter fields like gauze across a wound. A flock of birds sat in the branches of a low tree, as though stranded there by a high white tide. I yawned and rested my head against the glass. I'd been up until late, talking with Hutchins. He planned to return the following evening, to hear how I'd got on with Parrish, and to formulate a plan of action as far as the house was concerned. When I looked again, the birds and the tree were gone, as though conjured away, and the mist held nothing for a moment.

There was an odd item in my *Guardian* that morning. It meant nothing at the time, but I remembered it later. Six people in Bloomsbury had been admitted to hospital suffering from a mysterious condition. The first sign had been sudden blindness, striking without warning as the victims went about their daily routines. One man in his fifties had gone blind while driving, and had crashed his car into a lamp-post, suffering minor injuries. None of the victims were related. A consultant at the Middlesex Hospital said that the cause of the illness was unknown and that the victims would be kept in hospital for observation. So far, none had recovered their sight.

A taxi left me at Pembroke. Alice, told which train I'd be arriving on, was waiting near the porter's lodge. Her blonde hair was tied back in a bun, and she was dressed in a severely-cut black suit. Clearly, becoming a fellow had changed her style.

'Very grown up,' I ventured.

She frowned and leaned forward, kissing me on both cheeks.

'Don't be cheeky. Everyone grows out of jeans some time.'

I looked down at my blue-clad legs and sighed.

'Not even on a dig?'

Alice had been my tutee at Manchester, and we'd spent several seasons at digs in eastern Turkey. We'd never actually slept together, but there had been a thing between us, something rather more than friendship. I'd been keen on pursuing something physical, but she'd backed off and we'd continued friends. I wondered if she could tell me Peter Lazenby's secret. How did a middle-aged man with cranky ideas and a lecherous mind manage to persuade so many women between his sheets?

She took my arm and led me back out onto Trumpington Street.

'Especially not on digs,' she said. 'Come on, we're going this way.'

We got a taxi in St Andrew's Street. Nick Parrish lived on a small farm at Stow Cum Quy.

'Nick had a breakdown while he was out in Iraq,' she said. 'But I expect you know that already.'

'A little. What was the department told?'

'Just that—that he'd had a breakdown. No explanation, just a letter from his psychiatrist at Fulbourn asking that he be excused work on the grounds of clinical condition number such-and-such. He was in there about three months. I visited a few times, but he hardly knew me. He'd picked up a bit by the time he left, but his girlfriend didn't want him having anything to do with his old job. She's a potter, has a kiln at this farm. Her name's Sarah Jones-Hornsby. Very pukkah. We've all been warned off. She says she doesn't want anything reminding him of whatever it was sparked off this thing in the first place.'

'What does he do now?'

'I haven't the foggiest. Sits down and stares out the window all day for all any of us know.'

The taxi turned into a rutted lane, swinging past an open gate that held a hand-painted sign reading 'Stow Pottery. Fine ceramics to order. Raku a speciality.' The lane turned to the right, and five hundred yards more took us to the main building. Outhouses stood a little further on. The rest was open field.

I paid the taxi and took his telephone number for the return trip. Stepping back as he drove away, I felt suddenly abandoned. I looked round. The farmhouse was a sturdy building of two storeys, with little to commend it but its sturdiness. And its isolation, if that's what mattered. Paint peeled from the door and window-frames, mortar had fallen away from brick like filling matter from a rotten tooth. The surroundings were equally bleak. Old farms turned to other uses are curiously depressing, as though the spirit has departed from them. I expected to hear cows low or chickens stutter, and instead heard the tinny whine of a transistor radio from somewhere deep inside the farmhouse. A curious silence clung to the fields.

Alice knocked on the door. It had been her idea to turn up without prior warning, on the grounds that, if I was on her doorstep, Sarah would find it harder to turn me away. I wasn't so sure.

The door opened to reveal a pretty woman of about thirty, dressed in a long apron, her dark hair cut short, and one cheek smeared with potter's clay. She smiled entrancingly.

'Yes? Are you looking for the pottery?'

'Not as such. My name's Alice Bird. You may remember me—we met a while ago. At Fulbourn.'

The smile vanished.

'I told you to stay away from here. You and your friends. Nick's getting on fine, he doesn't want you lot showing up here and reminding him of things he wants to forget.'

'I only came to see how he is. You can't cut him off from his past completely. We're all very concerned. He has friends who haven't seen him in well over a year.'

'That's none of my concern.' With a frown cut through her features, Sarah no longer looked as pretty as I'd at first thought. 'All I care about is making sure he's safe.'

'Can't we see him for just a few minutes? I've brought someone here who's come all the way from London.'

'I don't care if he just got in from Outer Mongolia, he's wasting his time.'

At that moment, there was a movement behind her, and a thin man of about thirty-five appeared. He looked pale and sickly. If he was getting better, I wondered how he'd been. I began to wonder if I was doing the right thing, if Sarah wasn't perhaps correct to keep him away from all contact with anything that might upset him. Or was that what was keeping him so ill?

'Alice? Is that you?'

He came forward into the light. His eyes were preternaturally bright. I sensed the presence of strong drugs. His unshaven cheeks were hollow, and dark bags beneath his eyes spoke of long nights with little sleep.

Alice made to go towards him, but Sarah stepped between them.

'Go back in, Nick. I'll see she leaves.'

He took her arm and made to draw her aside, but she was stronger and knew how to hold her ground.

'I said go back in. She only came to ask how you were. I've told her, and she's leaving.'

Whatever Nick had been through, it had not entirely sapped his will. He kept his hand on Sarah's arm, pressing down on it until she gave in and let it drop.

'It's all right,' he said. 'I'm fit for visitors. Come in, Alice. Let her past, Sarah, she's not a stranger.'

Alice moved into the narrow breach that had opened between Sarah and the door, and at the last moment the other woman gave way and let her through.

'Nick, this is Tom Alton. You don't know him, but . . .'

'I know his name, though.' He looked at me, and interest struggled in his eyes. 'Manchester, isn't that right?'

I shook my head.

'Not any longer. I'm at the British Museum now, but, yes, I was at Manchester for a while.'

'Well, it's nice to meet you at last. Come on in. Sarah makes a lovely pot of tea. Don't you, dear?'

The look she gave him was a combination of anger, fear, and heart-rending love. I had to turn aside. There was a silent tussle, then Sarah admitted defeat.

'Half an hour,' she said. 'You'll overtire him otherwise.'

He showed us into a higgledy-piggledy sort of room, all chairs and sofas and throws, nothing matching, nothing new. The walls were thick with books, and all sorts of other objects had been crammed into the spaces between them and the shelves. Five or six cats, all grey, all silent, lurked in warm corners, eyeing us warily.

Sarah went off to make tea, still scowling. For the first time in God knows how many months, her protecting veil had been torn. I was sorry for her. She meant well; but the world could not be shut out for ever.

'What are you doing now, Nick?' Alice sat facing him on a pouffe covered in a dull red shawl. I noticed examples of what I took to be Sarah's work on the window sill and on tables here and there. Strong shapes wrapped in striking glazes. Not just bowls, but indefinable creations of no evident purpose that seemed to have come into being of their own accord.

'I help Sarah in the pottery. She's teaching me to throw.' He laughed uneasily, as though unaccustomed to doing so. 'I can't quite get the hang of it. But she says I will.'

Alice filled him in on the goings-on in the department, and talked about her own last dig, at Bogazköy in Turkey. Sarah brought a tray on which sat a teapot (one of her own, a thing of spirals and gentle flutings in a blue glaze) and cups. A plate held plain chocolate biscuits.

'Olivers,' I said. They were the most expensive biscuit available. They didn't fit in here, like the ceramics.

'They're Nick's favourites,' Sarah said, almost defensively. 'I do what I can.'

He reached out and caught her hand, and again there was a naked exchange of feeling. I felt such an intruder.

Alice turned to me.

'I'd like to talk to Sarah alone. Would you mind staying with Nick? I'm sure he'd like to hear about your new job.'

Before Sarah could protest too loudly, Alice had her by the arm and was steering her out of the room. I poured some tea and handed the cup to Nick. His hand shook as he carried it to his lap and rested it there. I offered him a biscuit.

'You've come about Babylon,' he said. 'To find out what happened there.'

'How do you know? You didn't even know I was coming today.'

'I don't sleep very much; but when I do, I dream. I had a dream last night. There was a blind woman in it, and a child, a boy of eight or nine. Do you know them?'

'My wife and her son,' I said. 'She's called Nicola. His name is Adam.'

'Adam Kadmon,' he said. 'Primal man.'

'The *Zohar*.' I was familiar with the Hebrew term, and where it came from, but that was about all.

He nodded.

'And earlier than that. He's not your son?'

I shook my head.

'His father is Jewish?'

'No, Arab. An Iraqi.'

'Ask your wife about the father. The boy is important.'

'Important?'

'I don't know how. In my dream he was important. Is your wife pregnant?'

I nodded.

'The baby is important as well. But I'm frightened for the boy. I sensed he was in danger.'

'You talk as though . . .'

'As though I know more than I should? In a way. I told you, I have dreams when all I want is sleep. I see things when all I want to do is forget. So, yes, I know more than I should.'

'What happened at Babylon?'

I felt a silence grow between us. He looked scared and lonely.

'Didn't Monelli tell you?'

I shook my head.

'Monelli's dead.'

That seemed to shock him. The teacup tottered on his lap, and I leaned forward to take it. As I did so I noticed his wrists, the barely healed scars. He looked at me and made no attempt to drop his sleeves. I gave him the details of Ed's death, and he listened in silence.

'I have his journal,' I said. And I told him what I'd read there.

'Do you believe it? That I saw Lazenby and Caroline?'

I told him I'd no reason to disbelieve him, that I'd seen enough in my own house to rub away all suspicion. He nodded, reassured. My disbelief would have hurt him badly.

'I was never given to—what do you want to call them? Psychic experiences? Ghosts, poltergeists, possessions—there was nothing like that in my past. I was brought up a sceptic and remained one until the moment Maurice Price told me Peter Lazenby was dead. At the time I said nothing. I didn't want to make a fool of myself, so I just pretended I must have been mistaken, that I'd seen another old man and taken him for someone who was now dead. But I hadn't made a mistake.'

His hands twisted slowly on one another like cogs with their teeth cruelly intermeshed.

'I knew Peter Lazenby quite well, you see. He was the fount of all wisdom in my field, and I used to visit him once or twice a week while I was doing my Ph.D. We never became close friends. There was something about him I never could like, and I felt uncomfortable in the house. Now I think I understand why. Anyway, I'd never have mistaken him.'

'Why didn't you approach him that time?'

'At the dig? He was a little bit off, and someone had just come up with a heap of work that needed urgent attention. I thought I'd catch him at dinner.'

'What else happened? Did you see anything else?'

'I saw Lazenby again. He was down by the infill, where Caroline and her party had been working. I was struck by the fact that he no longer seemed blind. I watched him for a long time, but I couldn't pick up the courage to approach him.'

'No, I can quite understand that. What was he doing?'

'Walking round and round. He seemed impatient. He kept bending down and touching the ground, as though he wanted to take something from it but couldn't. Then . . .'

Nick's face went pale.

'It's all right,' I said. 'You don't have to . . .'

'No, I'll tell you. I must have made a movement. He looked round and caught sight of me. Of course, he couldn't have recognized me, he'd never seen me before, even though we'd spent so much time together. But he looked straight at me, and it was as if . . . It was like an animal, not a human being. Just for a few moments, then he blinked and his eyes seemed human again.

'Just then Caroline and Abdul-Ghaffar turned up. They just went straight down to where they'd left off working, and didn't so much as glance in Lazenby's direction. They couldn't have missed him, they were within inches of him. When I looked again, he was gone.'

I looked at him. He'd started shaking. I wondered how long I could press him before he broke again.

'Is this what made you ill?' I asked. 'Seeing Lazenby like that?'

He shook his head.

'No. Something . . . happened that night. Whispering . . . in my sleep. Lazenby's voice, then another voice . . . An ugly voice, speaking a language I didn't understand. When I woke, the whispering was still there and . . . I put on the light. Lazenby was there, near the entrance. Looking at me. And there was something with him.'

'Something . . .?'

'Its face was . . .'

He stood up, agitated. His voice had risen, alerting Sarah. The door opened and she entered, trailing Alice.

'That's enough!' she snapped, running to him and putting her arms round him protectively. 'I said he wasn't to be disturbed. Do you realize what he's been through, what he's still going through?'

There was nothing I could say. My quest for information could hardly be set beside his need for sanity, or her love for him. We made bumbling apologies and left, leaving Sarah to soothe her broken lover as best she could. I felt tainted and ashamed. But I was beginning to understand a little more. Just before Sarah entered, Nick had said something else. 'It had wings,' he'd said.

'Black wings like silk.'

Chapter Twenty

Nicola's Journal continued:

3 February

I tried the kill the baby today. It's been growing so fast lately that I've become quite terrified of it. I heard it laughing yesterday. Not a gurgling or a cooing that you might expect from a little baby, but something quite adult and not very nice. It whispers too, I can hear it, as if there's someone else in there with it. So I made my mind up to kill it, before it grows too strong.

What I wanted was to bring about a miscarriage, then let them handle the rest at the hospital. They'd have no choice about an abortion then. It seemed so simple, I thought it would all be over by this evening. I hadn't reckoned on the baby, on what he's already capable of.

Taken in large doses, the herb wormwood will cause the uterus to contract. My mother told me to avoid it, because I'd been using herbal remedies when pregnant with Adam. I ordered some on Tuesday, after returning from the hospital. A shop in Kensington sends herbs by post. The man who handled my order asked, 'Are you pregnant?' 'No,' I said, 'I'm blind.' He took it as an honest answer, as though blindness precludes childbearing. The handicapped don't have sex, the blind can't bring up children. They'd sterilize us if they could.

The wormwood arrived two days ago, but I didn't have the courage to use it right away. I made a braille label for it and kept it in a drawer in the kitchen, and from time to time I went there, fingering the bottle as an alcoholic might stroke a jar of whiskey, saving it for later, like a treat long promised.

The things that happened while Tom was away made my mind up for me. I thought, for no reason other than my fear of the thing, that getting rid of whatever had taken up residence in my womb might serve to remove the sounds and visions that haunted me that night. I can believe anything of the baby, you see: that it has the power to summon up something dark and fluttering from the recesses of the house itself.

No, I don't quite mean that. I think the house is nothing more than a sounding-board or a camera. It picks up or amplifies whatever darknesses lie at a deeper level. I know all about darkness, I have seen nothing else for almost twenty years. The house is built around something very old, something that has been trying to emerge for a long, long time.

The baby knows all about it. The baby is in tune with its moods and its needs. One reinforces the other, the darkness and the baby, and whatever is still to come. The Son of Shabbatil. The Demon Pazuzu. Whatever is still to come.

I can believe anything of the thing in my womb. It communicates, and I dread to think what it communicates with. I think it listens, even when I am asleep.

I made up my mind last night, but waited till this morning, when Tom was at work and Adam at school. I thought it would be safer that way. I don't trust Adam. He and the baby communicate in some way.

When they were gone, I cleared away the breakfast things, slowly and carefully, as I always do. I took my time. I made myself another cup of tea, and sat with it, thinking through what I intended. There was a risk that I might do myself some permanent damage. Some people think herbal remedies are mild, and I suppose they are in proper doses. I intended to drink the entire bottle, just to be sure, but I'd no idea what else that might do to me.

How did I intend to explain it to everyone, to the

hospital staff, to Tom, to my parents? It wouldn't have been difficult. We blind women make mistakes of that kind all the time, don't we?

When I'd finished my tea, I rinsed my cup and left it on the draining board to dry. I hated being in the house on my own, but I had no choice. Anyway, I wasn't really alone, was I?

I knew I was trying to spin things out, but no one likes to take an irrevocable step without thinking it over, or pretending to. Perhaps that was my mistake. Perhaps, if I'd acted sooner. . . . I'll never know. I went upstairs to tidy the bedrooms, then I took a shower. Standing under the cascade of hot water, I started to rub my hand back and forwards across my belly. I felt swollen beyond all that was natural. I was sure I could feel the baby move, as though the friction of my hand passing over him brought him to life. I tried to speak to him, but he wasn't interested. He has his own friends. Nintu the birth-goddess. Pashittu, the demon who snatches the newly-born from their mother's laps. All the gods and demons of Babylon.

It must have been ten o'clock or later by the time I settled down sufficiently to get the bottle. I took it from the drawer and put it on the table, then I went and found a glass. I'd read that wormwood is extremely bitter, so I thought I'd make it more palatable with some sort of juice. There was some apple juice in the fridge. I put some of the wormwood in the glass and slowly topped it up with juice. Another ten minutes passed before I touched the glass again. I gave the mixture a quick stir, then took a sip.

Even now I'm not sure exactly what happened. No sooner had I taken the wormwood on my tongue—and it was extraordinarily bitter, juice or not—than the glass was knocked flying from my hand and went smashing against the wall opposite. Something grabbed me from behind, something rough and hard, and I heard a loud fluttering, as though I was surrounded by immense wings, as if the room was suddenly filled with them.

The next thing I knew, I was lying on my back on the cold kitchen floor.

The fluttering stopped as quickly as it had begun. I'd lost my bearings completely, didn't know which way was which. Dimly, I could hear Benjie barking from the next room, where I'd left him. I struggled to right myself, but the floor was slippery with wormwood, and I caught my hand on a shard of splintered glass, cutting my palm right across.

'Stand up.'

I recognized the voice at once. Lazenby's voice. Not dark and insinuating as before, but stern and cold. I had never heard a voice more devoid of warmth.

'I can't get up,' I said. 'The floor's a mess.'

'You can stand up now,' he said. 'The floor is dry.'

I reached out a hand and swept the surface of the marble tiles. The wormwood had gone. Painfully, I got to my knees, then, shaking, to my feet. I felt myself surrounded, but I did not know by what. Somewhere, in a corner, I heard a murmur of leathery wings. And something else. Like a large animal opening and closing its jaws.

'You were warned,' he said. 'Your son warned you.'

'Warned me?'

'Against harming the child.'

'He's not a child. I don't know what he is, but he's not human.'

'On the contrary, he's more truly human than any of us. He's a perfect being. You're privileged to carry him. And very foolish to attempt to harm him.'

'I'll do it again.' It was bravado, but what else did I have at that moment? Inwardly, I was shaking like a baby bird torn from the nest.

'No, you will never try anything like that again. Believe me.'

'I'll go to the hospital. I'll insist . . .'

'"And the name of the star is called Wormwood; and the third part of the waters became wormwood; and many men died of the waters, because they were made bitter." '

That was all he said. Later, I remembered where he'd taken the words from, the Book of Revelation. At the time, I was incapable of remembering anything, incapable even of thinking. My mouth filled with a taste vile beyond imagining. I tried to open my lips to spit it out, but they would not open, and I was forced to swallow. The bitter liquid rushed down to my stomach as though I'd swallowed a lump of coal, and my mouth filled up again, and again I was forced to swallow.

Within less than a minute I felt as though every vein in my body was drenched in the stuff. It wasn't real wormwood at all, of course: this wasn't going to harm the baby. But it poisoned me, making me cough and choke and gasp for breath until I was on my hands and knees, retching.

I don't know how long it went on. It felt like hours or days or months. I lost all sense of time. All I was conscious of was the bitterness filling me, eating at me, as though turning my flesh to wormwood.

Suddenly it stopped. It was like a prayer being answered. One moment, nothing but bitterness and absinth, the next a honeylike sweetness in all my veins. And then his voice came again.

'Open your eyes.'

I'd been keeping them tightly clenched. Now, like a puppet, utterly supine, I did as he commanded.

I must have passed out screaming. Tom found me there, hours later, when he returned from work. I can remember two things only from that moment before I lost consciousness: a winged figure with a tail staring down at me, and my own voice, crying for help.

Tom took me straight to the hospital. Adam was with Michael for the evening, a pre-arranged visit. They thought I was going to lose the baby at first, but after an hour or so of tests, a nurse came to my room, smiling and telling me there was nothing to worry about.

'Your baby's fine,' she said. 'Alive and kicking.

How many weeks is it now?'

I told her.

'You must be mistaken,' she said. 'You're out by over a month, I'd say. Either that or you know something your husband doesn't.'

I smiled reluctantly. I'd said nothing to Tom about the abortion attempt, nor had I any intention of saying anything.

Adam was waiting for me when I got home. When Tom left the room to fetch the morning paper, he came and stood next to me.

'You should have listened to me, mother,' he said in that dead voice of his. 'This could have been avoided. You won't try it again, will you?'

I shook my head. And somewhere deep inside me the baby kicked its little legs and laughed.

Chapter Twenty-one

I feared the worst when I found Nicola on the kitchen floor, but the hospital gave her the all clear and sent her home. What I was most afraid of was that she might remain concussed like Adam, and spend weeks hovering between life and death. The baby's fine, thank God. I know Nicola has some idea that the baby is a threat to us, but I draw the line there. The baby has nothing to do with whatever Peter Lazenby set in motion all those years ago.

Nobody has any explanation for what happened. Nicola herself is tight-lipped, and refuses to say anything about how she came to pass out. I found a broken bottle that had contained some strong-smelling liquid on the floor. She says it was herbal medicine to help with morning sickness, but I can't imagine how anything as foul-smelling as that could do anyone any good. I've warned her to take nothing except what Dr Hamilton prescribes. She nodded and said nothing. Whatever had been in the bottle had dried, otherwise I'd have taken a sample in to the hospital and got an opinion.

Andrew Hutchins came round about nine. Nicola was in bed, resting, and Adam was in his room, practising the flute. Andrew and I have been going through Lazenby's papers together. It's a tedious job, especially when we're not really sure exactly what we're looking for. I came across a whole box full of smutty photographs circa 1950. Some of them wouldn't get passed by a censor now, let alone close on fifty years ago. I think they were taken by Lazenby himself. All sorts of poses, none of them demure, and you could tell he'd had sex with them just before taking the photographs, or that he was planning to do so as soon as he put down the camera.

There was one odd thing on several of the shots. Some of the women were wearing what looked like a large medallion or a talisman round their necks, and Lazenby (or someone) had gone to the trouble of colouring this in with gold ink. The funny thing was that, in any photograph where the model was wearing the medallion, she'd have her eyes closed. Neither Andrew nor I could work out what it meant.

We made our first serious discovery about eleven o'clock, just as Andrew had started yawning and we were thinking of calling it a day.

'What's this?' he said, pulling out a large notebook. There were several more under it, all more or less identical: large blue notebooks with red cloth bindings, each about two hundred pages thick. Inside, they were filled with a thin scrawl that I recognized as Lazenby's hand. There were dates on the little white labels that adorned the front of each book, ranging from 1945 through to 1973. A quick dip inside confirmed that these were Lazenby's journals, a meticulous record of his life and work. If there were going to be any answers to the questions that perplexed us, they must surely be in those pages.

Andrew and I divided the journals between us. He took the earlier ones, I the later. We agreed to keep notes of anything particularly interesting, and to meet in a couple of days to compare our findings.

Nicola was fast asleep when I retired. I sat on the edge of the bed for a while, reading through the first journal. It must have been well after 2.00 when, exhausted and not a little bewildered, I finally turned out the light. Even then, sleep did not come readily. And when it came, my dreams were unsettling. Dark shapes crawled through them. I was walking through a city with high mud-brick walls and narrow passages between the buildings. Babylon, not as it is now, much levelled with the earth, but Babylon as it looked when Koldewey first excavated it, when Peter Lazenby first set eyes upon it as a young man in the late twenties. How did I know? Everywhere I went, a figure went ahead of me, tall and slim and dressed in European clothes. And sometimes, turning a corner, he would turn and smile back at me, a dreadful, knowing smile, and the face that I saw was the face I had seen in dozens of old photographs, arrogant and self-possessed. It was as if he wanted me to know the truth.

Chapter Twenty-two

From the Journal of Peter Lazenby:

22 May 1962

Another frustrating day with the Greeks. What a bunch of fools. Really. What they knew about Babylon was all moonshine and nonsense. They might as well have been a pub full of Irish fabulists for all the sense you can ever get out of them. The Romans are just as bad. I'm beginning to despair of getting any real knowledge from the Ancients. And so many of the Babylonian texts are fragmentary. A snippet here, a hint there, then a gap where the original tablet was snapped in two or crumbled. Fragments and broken words. I am near to despair.

29 May

Re-read Diodorus Siculus today, in Skelton's translation. Both he and Herodotus speak of golden images, of lions and serpents, and chambers of gold to keep them in. But nothing more than that, not even a hint. I'm more than ever convinced I'm looking in the wrong place.

12 June

Something turned up today by chance. My old friend Jacques Marat sent me a photocopy of a manuscript that turned up last week in the Bibliothèque Nationale. It had been bound with a volume of Tacitus and stuck on a shelf since 1726. It's only a fragment, of course: seventeen pages from the lost history of Assyria by the Greek physician Ctesias. Until now, we've only had access to a few passages in Diodorus Siculus. This is far from the whole thing, of course; but I've started reading it. Hope springs eternal.

14 June

Ctesias is disappointing on the whole. But there are two paragraphs that gives me heart. He was writing in the fifth century before Christ, before the great changes took place in Babylon.

I spoke yesterday with a priest of Marduk, their principal god, whose great temple stands in the south of the city, at the end of the Street of Processions, facing the Acropolis. There is, he said, a hidden place within the city, a sanctuary hidden beneath the earth, where none but a certain priesthood may gain admission. If any not of their number should venture there, he may not leave the place again, but must surrender his life at the foot of the black god that stands in the inmost of those dark chambers.

He would not tell me what manner of god it was that inhabited this sanctuary, nor what name they call him by, but he spoke in hushed tones and forbade me to mention any of this afterwards. It is also said that should a woman among them be widowed when young, and find favour with the priests of this god, she must go to that place under oath, and expose herself before the god's image. And if she should have a male child, it shall be considered the son of the god. Whether the woman is permitted to live after this, he would not say.

4 July

American Independence Day. What a meaningless concept. Political freedom means nothing without spiritual strength. The Americans, like the Europeans before them, have lost all their virility. The most powerful nation on earth, yet there is no one there who can distinguish reality from dream, substance from mist.

I had the dream of Shabbatil last night. He shows himself to me now as a winged demon with a horned head. The Lord of Flies. The Master of Darkness. Satan. I am beginning to understand what he says. The last words I heard as I was beginning to awake were: *Shabbatil ipal*—Shabbatil will answer.

20 August

My tickets for Baghdad arrived today. It's frustrating to have been so tied up that I have to make this year's visit late in the vacation. The political situation over there isn't exactly calm, but there's no point in waiting till it settles down.

Two prospective undergraduates turned up for interview today. Neither very bright, but both extremely nubile. I promised them firm places, and they seemed grateful. One smelt like a virgin; the other has seen a little action. It promises to be an eventful year. The virgin is the daughter of Lord G—, which makes her something of a double challenge. Aristocratic pussy has an unusally silky touch.

Baghdad
17 September

Five days in this wretched city, and still nothing. I have visited every bookshop in the city, but without success. Manuscripts in profusion, but nothing that comes close. They all look at me as though I'm a little odd, and perhaps I am.

A tall figure followed me through the suq today. He was dressed in a black robe. His face was always in shadow when I turned, whether he stood in light or shade, it made no difference. He knew I was aware of him. I did not turn back or wait for him, but kept on walking. I cannot yet be sure if what I summoned is the right one. If I have made a mistake . . .

Baghdad
19 September

Hasan at the Museum gave me the name of a bookbinder in the Suq al-'Attarin. His name is Marwan, and they say he was a Jew originally. Now, however, he's as pious a Muslim as can be found in the city, and a mine of information. People bring their books to him to be bound in leather, and he acts as a go-between for book collectors and scholars.

His shop was in the Old City, a dark, airless place where the men speak in whispers and the women glide like veiled ghosts, making their purchases with gestures, as though a plague had struck them dumb. The Caliph Harun al-Rashid used to walk these streets, just as it says in the Thousand and One Nights. Perhaps it was romantic then; not now.

I got lost more than once in a maze of twisting alleyways and narrow culs-de-sac. Everywhere I went, I found fast-closed doorways and heavily shuttered windows. I sensed eyes watching me pass from behind the lattices, women and girls and old men. They understand the power of sex here: it's a force so strong, it must be veiled, locked up behind strong doors, hemmed in by high walls. The moment you remove the veil, it bursts forth like an explosion.

It took me over an hour to find the shop, a cramped little den at the back of a courtyard full of sacks containing sesame seeds, fenugreek, and other spices. The smell was almost overpowering at times. Every inch of wall-space was taken up by shelves, each shelf packed with books. The only light came from an opening high in the ceiling and from an oil lamp beside which Marwan worked, stitching his bindings on his lap, which he covered with a leather apron.

I spoke with him for above an hour, telling him that I wanted to know about Babylon. He's a man of sixty or more, wizened, long-bearded, bespectacled, with penetrating eyes that seem to look right into you. At the end, he told me all the usual things: read Ya'qubi read Tabari, read Mas'udi. I said I had read them all, and all there was in Greek and Latin, but what I wanted was not to be found there. He shrugged and murmured that, in that case, there was nothing more he could do for me, and turned back to his sewing.

I was about to leave when I made up my mind to show him the tablet. It was in a pouch in my pocket. Perhaps it's foolish of me to carry it about on my person: it could get broken or crushed. But I know it by heart now, the tablet itself is no more than evidence of its own existence.

'Where did you find this?' he asked, taking a renewed interest in me the moment I produced it. He must have seen a thousand fakes in his time. How did he know this one was genuine?

'On an expedition to Babylon,' I said. 'Ten years ago.'

'There was no expedition ten years ago.'

'You're very well informed.'

'I have eyes and ears like anyone. It pays to look and listen. Where did you find this tablet?'

I watched his eyes scrutinizing me as though I was a volume he was preparing to bind. A little bell rang at the rear of the shop, and I caught sight of a small boy, eight or nine years old, pale faced and attractive. He came up to the old man and whispered in his ear. Marwan nodded, and the boy went out again, ringing the little bell as he went. The old man's eyes went to my face again.

'Someone brought it back from the Koldewey expedition,' I said. 'It was a long time ago. 1904 or 1905, I think. That was when they were excavating the eastern portion of Nabopolassar's palace. They found a large coffin made of pottery.'

'Yes, I know of it. Some say it belonged to Nabopolassarr himself. That his son Nebuchadnezzar laid him to rest there.'

'That's possible. Anyway, they found some gold plates in the rubbish around the sarcophagus—some circles, some rectangles. Near them were some clay tablets with cuneiform inscriptions. One of the diggers found a way to remove several of each without anyone else knowing. I found them in Paris during the war, in an antique shop on the rue Mouffetard. They'd been sold to the dealer by a German soldier. That's all I know.'

Marwan weighed the tablet in his hand, as though assessing its true value.

'Can you read it?' he asked.

'I wouldn't be here otherwise.'

'Read it to me.'

Outside, darkness had started to fall over the Old City, as though a pall of smoke was descending on its walls and streets and alleyways. I felt nervous about making my way back to my hotel through that unlit labyrinth. The sound of the call to evening prayer came rippling from a dozen mosques. I thought Marwan would interrupt our conversation, tell me to wait while he performed his ablutions and made his devotions. But he kept his eyes expectantly on me, and I sensed that he knew more than he revealed. In the little courtyard, someone was playing a pipe very softly. Its music moved intricately alongside the voice of the muezzin. I wondered if the music came from the boy I had seen.

I took the tablet from Marwan's open hand. I wondered if I could trust him. He was, after all, a total stranger. I'd already revealed the existence of the tablet to him, but its contents were known only to myself. I looked down at the wedge-shaped marks that formed the text and made up my mind.

I took a deep breath. I had never read the tablet aloud before.

'*Unium lidda-im li-tur likil,*' I read. The ancient words seemed to hover in the lamp-lit air, blending with the chanting from the mosques and the lilting of the reed pipe.

Let the day become dark, Let it grow gloomy again. Death came to Babylon in the second year of the great king's reign. The beginning of it was blindness that took away a man's sight between sleep and waking, and the end of it a fever with great thirst that ended always in death. There was no street without widows, no quarter without orphans. The cry of mourning went up from Babil, and the sound of weeping from Imgur-bel.

On the seventh day, our Lord the King went to the Temple of Marduk, and there went with him all the priests of the city, and did penance. But the Lady Erishkigal, the Queen of the Realm of the Dead, only laughed at all their prayers, and sent the demon Namtar to bring more of the living within her power.

And when seven more days had passed, and the king had gone to all the gods for protection, and none had answered, he was persuaded to go alone to the dark place of Erishkigal, which is in Kish. And he entered there clad in sackcloth, and in the darkest of its dark chambers, he came upon the sha'ilu, *the questioner of the dead. And seven days and seven nights he remained in that place, and the* sha'ilu *brought forth the shades of the newly dead and questioned them.*

On the last day, the king was brought to a hidden chamber, where there was a statue of the great demon Shabbatil, that had been there since time began. The sha'ilu *instructed him to build a shrine in which to place the statue, and to offer sacrifices before it, a child from every household. Nabopolassar returned with a heavy heart to the city, fearing what evils might come once they had brought the Dark One among themselves.*

In Babylon, a habitation was built for the idol, and eyes of alabaster were placed there, that they might be witnesses of what was done. When this was finished, the statue of Shabbatil was set up therein. They brought the children there, but none of the priests would take a knife to slay them, neither the priests of Marduk, nor the priests of Shamash, nor the priests of Ishtar, nor any man among them. But that day there came to the gates of the city a man of Sippar to say that he had been sent to perform the sacrifice. On his feet he wore sandals of fine leather, and in his hand he carried a staff with a golden head in the image of Shabbatil.

With him there came a child of seven, a boy, the Son of Shabbatil. While the man of Sippar slew the children of the city, the boy sat beside him and played music on a pipe. Above seven hundred died, a child from every household, and the wailing of women was heard on the rooftops after that for forty days and forty nights . . .

I put down the tablet. My hand was shaking.

'It breaks off there,' I said.

The old man just looked at me in silence. Behind him the bell rang, and I saw the shadow of the boy as he entered and went out again.

'The man of Sippar was called Addu,' Marwan said.

'How do you know that?'

He stood up and went into another room. I waited, breathing the scent of paper and leather, mixed with spices. In the courtyard, the piping continued, though the call to prayer had ended.

When Marwan returned, he was holding a leather bag carefully in one hand. He opened it and took out a flat object wrapped in paper. He unwrapped it and held it towards me, letting it catch the little light that streamed from the lamp. It was a rectangle of gold. I held it nearer the light. The gold had been embossed with two figures: a winged demon, horned and staring, and a man holding a long staff. The cuneiform inscription beneath the demon read 'Shabbatil', and that beneath the man 'Addu of Sippar'.

'You want to find the statue,' Marwan said.

'Yes. Do you think it's possible?'

'Perhaps. I have seen documents. Give me a little time. Three days. Come back then, and I will give you whatever I can find.'

The streets were dark, and I lost my way several times on my way back. I wondered if I would ever find Marwan's little shop again. Twice, I looked back. The man in dark robes was following me. Each time I see him now, he is more solid. He carries a long staff in his right hand.

Chapter Twenty-three

Andrew gave me the name of the woman who'd been traumatized by Lazenby. I wanted to know what had happened. Had Lazenby been little more than a creep preying on vulnerable young women, or had there been more to it? He'd wanted to become a god—hadn't he said as much to Andrew and a few others? Were his sexual adventures part of that programme, or just a diversion?

Her name was Linda Turner, and she lived in a little flat in Clerkenwell, a few doors down from the post office, where she still worked. Andrew had visited her there a few times. I think he'd felt some sort of responsibility for her, knowing Lazenby as he did. She'd never told him the truth, never unburdened herself of whatever it was she still carried from those old days. I don't know why I thought I could do better. But I needed to know what drove him.

She was an attractive woman in her fifties, but spinsterish, as though she'd taken all her cues from an earlier generation of unmarried women. On opening the door, she swallowed me in a single glance. A capable woman, but tired. She could be tough all the same, I knew it right away. She'd made some sort of life for herself, but she probably wasn't sure what it amounted to. It occurred to me that I hadn't enquired of Andrew whether she had any interests outside her job. A choir, perhaps, or evening classes.

'You must be Andrew Hutchins's friend.'

I nodded.

'We work together at the museum,' I said. 'Well, not quite together: he's Middle Eastern antiquities, I'm Mesopotomia.'

'Well, you don't look it.' A flash of a smile, then she stood aside to let me in.

She'd been expecting me, I'd spoken briefly with her on the telephone the evening before, after Andrew warned her I might ring. Her voice then had been wary, as though she was unaccustomed to strangers. Or perhaps too familiar with them. Now she seemed more relaxed. But I still sensed a screen between us, like one of those glass partitions behind which she passed so much of her days.

'I've made a cake,' she said. 'Would you prefer tea or coffee?'

'Tea will be fine,' I said. 'Unless . . .'

'Lapsang, Darjeeling, or Earl Grey?' she asked.

'Earl Grey. With lemon if . . .'

She went off to a little kitchen and busied herself with a kettle and teapots. I looked round the living room. Some prints of Persian miniatures, a fine example of Arabic calligraphy, photographs of an eastern city, Cairo, perhaps, or Damascus.

'We used to call it Early Grey at home,' she said, bringing in two pots on a tray, both Wedgwood. 'Of course, nobody much drank it in those days except us queer folk.'

She poured tea and sliced cake with the air of a practised hostess. Yet I sensed that I was a rare visitor, that her tea and cakes were more often than not reserved for herself. A grey cat sat motionless on the back of her armchair, watching me through half-closed eyes.

'You studied Arabic?' I said, trying to nudge her towards the path I wanted to travel.

'For a couple of years,' she said. 'Far from long enough to master French or Italian, let alone a difficult language like that, but I learned a little, yes.'

'It can't have been popular in those days. And for a woman . . .'

'Oh, I don't know about that. There have been plenty of us women involved in the Middle East. Hester Stanhope, Gertrude Bell, Jane Dieulafoy in Persia . . . A tough old bunch.'

'Was that your inspiration?'

'Sort of. It was the Sixties, I was very idealistic, and I thought Arabic was the coming thing. I'd been a linguist at school, and it seemed a way to break away from the inevitable Latin, Greek, or modern languages.'

'But you didn't take your degree.'

She passed me a plate with dark chocolate cake on it. I took a bite.

'Delicious,' I said. 'You made it?'

'My mother taught me to make what she called the "Five Essential Things": a good cup of tea, a properly tossed salad, meat and lightly cooked vegetables, jam roly-poly, and chocolate cake. She said it would come in handy.' She stopped to take a deep breath before continuing. 'Well, it has done from time to time. I'm on my own mostly. I eat from hand to mouth. Andrew said you were married.'

'Yes. In a way that's why I'm here.'

'He said your wife is blind.'

'Yes. We have a son. At least, the boy is hers by an earlier marriage.'

'And how does that bring you here?'

'I think we may all have something . . . someone in common.'

She put her own plate down, the cake on it untouched. Behind her, the cat rose and stretched, opening its mouth wide to reveal gleaming white teeth and a red mouth.

'Peter Lazenby,' she said. She spoke the name as a priest might pronounce the word 'abortion', or a sceptic 'astrology'.

'What can you tell me about him?'

'Very little. I was taught by him. He was my tutor. I saw nothing more of him after I left the university. I should think you have access to dozens of people who knew him intimately. Why come to me?'

'I think you know. Andrew told me about the scandal that led to his being . . .'

'Reprimanded? He'd have been dismissed nowadays, of course. Back then, all they wanted to do was hush it up.'

'They could have dismissed him even then.'

'But they chose not to. They were almost all men. I think a few of them were envious.'

'Envious?'

'That he'd had sex with so many of his students. Most of them wanted to, but hadn't the guts or the skill. Some of us were very attractive young women. Lazenby had his pick.'

'Why was that?'

'He was good looking.'

'Lots of lecturers are good looking.'

'Fewer than you suppose. Well, where I was anyway?' She smiled, and for a moment I think she was remembering those two bright years, before things went wrong.

'Lazenby was persuasive. He had a seductive manner. It was hard to say no to him.'

'What else?'

I saw her freeze up.

'There was nothing else. He got found out, I left the university, he was reprimanded. I don't expect it did his love life much harm.'

'But you chose to leave. No one made you. Why was that?'

'Dr Alton, this is a very private matter. You come for tea, you make some small talk, and next thing you want to know all the details of my private life.'

'Hardly that,' I said. 'Surely what you told the committee . . .'

She shook her head briskly.

'Please, this is bringing back painful memories. I should have known better than to agree to meet with you. I thought you wanted to ask about Lazenby himself.'

She got to her feet abruptly. In her agitation, she sent her cup flying. It crashed on the floor, spilling tea across her skirt and the carpet. I jumped up, trying to help clear the mess, but she brushed me aside and dashed for the kitchen, returning with a damp cloth. She bent down and mopped up the little amber pool, then picked up the fragments of her cup. Getting to her feet again, she looked at me. There were tears in her eyes.

'I think you'd better go,' she said. 'You've caused enough trouble.'

'Please,' I said. 'This is important. My wife and our boy . . . Their lives may be at risk. Mine too, perhaps.'

'I don't understand. Your lives? Peter Lazenby's dead, he . . .'

I saw the colour drain from her face. Her hand started for her mouth, but she stopped herself half-way. I could see her fighting for control.

'I . . . think you'd better explain.'

It took a long time. My tea was cold well before I finished. Outside, the light had leached from the sky. I told her what I knew, what I suspected, what I feared. I risked her ridicule; but somehow I knew she would not make fun of me, or treat what I told her as fantasy. The more I watched her, the more certain I grew that I was not the first.

When I came to an end, she said nothing. She got up and took the teapots to the kitchen, one for Darjeeling, one for Earl Grey, and she put fresh water in the kettle and boiled it.

'Perhaps you'd like something stronger,' she said, coming back with hot tea and fresh cups on a tray.

'This is fine,' I said, and cut myself a fresh slice of lemon.

'He used to make tea for me,' she said. 'He was a kind man, or he appeared so. So many of our teachers kept themselves aloof. Peter never did. He'd make tea and sandwiches—cucumber, egg and cress, sometimes even smoked salmon, which was a real treat in those days. I looked forward to our tutorials all through the first year. We'd have our tea and chat about anything but work. I thought he took me seriously, that he considered me an adult. Perhaps he did. Anyway, it flattered me. Afterwards, we'd go over Arabic verbs. That was the nasty part. If you haven't studied them, you can't imagine what they're like. Hollow verbs, weak verbs, quadriliteral verbs . . .' She gave a little shudder. I nodded in sympathy. Assyrian wasn't any better.

'Usually, that was all. Verbs, or a translation, and later on a simple essay. I don't think I was very good, but he was patient, and I began to think I might get somewhere. But sometimes he'd get the grammar out of the way and move on to other subjects. He knew such a lot, I was in awe of him. I hadn't been to the Middle East then, but he used to tell me stories about it, about the cities, and the tribes, and the desert. He fascinated me. I started to think I was in love with him.'

She paused, blushing. I guessed that Peter Lazenby had been her first and last love.

'He talked a lot about what he called his philosophy. I can't remember much of it now. There was a lot about the Babylonians, how their religion was the original, the most authentic, how their gods were symbols for another reality, that if one could rediscover their rituals and use them as they were meant to be used, one could gain enlightenment.'

She swallowed some tea and put her cup back gently on its saucer. It was a perfect match for the one I had caused her to break.

'I don't suppose that would mean a lot now,' she went on. 'I hate to use the term "young people". Makes me sound an old frump. But it's true. All they seem to want is raves and ecstasy tablets and casual sex. Well, we did all that in the Sixties too, but it wasn't all we thought about. We were into love and flower power and the Maharishi. Some of us thought we could change the world. Peter Lazenby sounded as plausible as Timothy Leary or Krishnamurti. And he was there, inches away from me.'

She smiled, seeing herself eighteen again.

'I didn't wear cardigans back then,' she said. 'You wouldn't have recognized me. I was away from home, I was a virgin, I thought I had a soul. All I had to do was take my clothes off and do whatever Peter asked me to, and I'd be on my way. He offered me everything in a neat package: love, sex, enlightenment, adulthood.

'I used to think the little rituals were just an elaborate ruse, an imaginative means of getting young women into bed. Now I'm not so sure. He believed in what he was doing. The sex wasn't for its own sake. He used it to get energy. Even after we were going to bed together two or three times a week, he never stopped the rituals. I didn't care. I'd never been so happy in my life.

'I started staying the night. Not very often at first, then more frequently. Of course, I found out later he was seeing other women, other students at the same time. He had an incredible sexual energy. I've never been with another man since, but I'm not a total innocent. Even post office clerks read books and see films. Peter Lazenby had more energy than ten men put together.

'It was when I stayed with him that things began to go wrong. What you've told me . . . about your house, Lazenby's house—I've already seen and heard most of it. The bell, that smell of spices, a presence moving from room to room. The sex was part of it. Often, when we made love, he'd cry out in what I think was Babylonian. And, sometimes, something would come.'

'Something . . .?'

She was pale again. The fear had not left her in all these years.

'Please . . . I can't talk about it. I was alone in the house sometimes, and I . . . could hear things moving about. When I told him about it, he said I shouldn't be frightened, that we were bringing powerful spirits to life.'

'Did he ever mention something called Shabbatil?'

At first I thought she was not going to answer. Then she stood.

'Let me have a moment,' she said, then left the room.

When she came back, she was carrying a cardboard tube. She sat down and busied herself removing the lid, which had been stuck down with sellotape. From the tube she took a large sheet of thick paper.

'I found this in a drawer,' she said. 'He used to make drawings of me when I was asleep. This one . . . I kept it in case it would ever be needed.'

'Needed?'

'I'm not sure. By the police. I didn't know, I just kept it. The woman is me. My hair was longer then.'

She passed it to me. I made room on the table and unrolled it carefully. Over the years, the paper had grown fragile. The drawing had been done in black ink. Lazenby had been a skilful artist.

It showed a woman on a bed, naked, her hair spread across the sheet. Above her, also naked, his penis erect, knelt a second figure. The Great Demon Shabbatil, his wings folded above him, and his tail coiled on his back.

Chapter Twenty-four

I finished my volumes of Lazenby's journal more quickly than I'd originally expected, taking time off work in order to get to the end. They simultaneously fascinated and repelled me. I scarcely ate or drank in that time, so immersed was I in what I read. By the time I was halfway through I'd lost my appetite anyway. For whom had Lazenby kept such a detailed record of his thoughts and doings, I wondered. Himself? A successor?

Marwan the bookbinder turned out to be an asset beyond Lazenby's wildest dreams. Over the next few years, he tracked down all manner of documents, most of them in Arabic, some in Hebrew, some in Greek. Bit by bit, the pieces of the puzzle moved into place. A reference here, a hint there, an allusion somewhere else—they all began to mean something.

Either he had been looking for the demon Shabbatil, or Shabbatil himself had been in search of him: it makes little or no difference. Shabbatil was in Babylon—but where? It was a vast place, the greatest city of the ancient world. Could Peter Lazenby, who was not, after all, a trained archaeologist, find what generations of professionals had missed?

He began to think he could. He had something most of them lacked: a knowledge of classical Arabic. The Arabs had lived around Babylon for centuries. They had taken bricks from the site to build Hilla, cultivated crops in the surrounding fields, and built villages on top of its ruins. Somewhere, Lazenby reasoned, there must be mention of things they had seen, things they had discovered.

Andrew came over the following evening as arranged. He had been ploughing his way through the early volumes, discovering the origins of Lazenby's twin obsessions: sex and eternal life. I gave him a full account of Linda's story, and showed him the drawing she had let me take away.

'She says she had sex with this? Surely that's impossible.'

I shrugged. All I had was her word. But I believed her. She dreamed of it every night, she said, so much that she was daily terrified of sleep. Somehow it always came, and every night as she slept she felt herself come awake within her dream, and it would be there, a winged shadow dipping and swaying above her.

'She says Lazenby drugged her. Told her he had access to acid, handed her a couple of tablets. She could remember very little afterwards. But once or twice there were cuts on her skin. He said she'd inflicted them on herself, while under the influence of the drug. They didn't heal properly, and she had to be treated at the hospital. She still has scars.'

We found a box containing everything Marwan had sold to Lazenby. The old man hadn't been lazy. There must have been a couple of hundred separate items, some of them scraps of paper, others leather-bound manuscripts. They all looked genuine. Had Marwan just been a good forger, or uncannily skilled at laying his hands on the sort of thing Lazenby was after?

Most of it was in Arabic. Andrew said he'd take it home and have a stab at translating what he could.

'Lazenby was exceptionally skilled,' he said. 'He could decipher the most difficult scripts in the worst handwriting. I used to bring things over for him to read, when none of us could make head nor tail of them. When he lost his sight it was a tragedy. I still have a file of unreadable texts in my office that he could have read like nobody's business.'

'This one looks difficult,' I said, holding out a sheet of darkened parchment covered in spidery writing. Andrew took it and held it to the light. I watched shadows from the gas fire thicken and dissolve on his hands. Outside, a wind had risen, lifting its head and strutting through the cold streets, rattling my window sashes, as though to keep the coming spring at bay.

Andrew took the document from me and looked at it closely, holding it sideways to the light. The shadows seemed to thicken as he did so. Something heavy rumbled through the street, carried by the wind.

'This isn't as difficult as it looks,' he said. 'From the look of it, it's an Abbasid chancellery hand from around the tenth century. The script's known as *tawqi'*. It was used for official documents. There aren't many examples from that period. They'd discovered paper by then, so most of what was written perished. This is on parchment. It's actually very well preserved.'

He read through it silently. I watched him, thinking of all the times he must have sat here, just like this, discussing such matters with Peter Lazenby—the finer points of scripts, the provenance of forgotten manuscripts. The more we talked, the more we read, the more we rifled through his papers, the stronger Lazenby's presence grew.

'I'll make a stab at it,' said Andrew. 'It seems quite interesting. It was written in Baghdad in—let's see—yes, in 930. That would have been the reign of al-Muqtadir.'

He began to read while at his back the wind roared and clattered, sometimes hard enough to drown his words.

'*In the Name of God, the Merciful, the Compassionate. Praise be to God, Lord of all the Worlds.*
I have looked upon the face of Satan . . .'

He read on, pausing at times to work out the meaning of a difficult passage, and I knew that, if I closed my eyes, I would see it all, the dark chamber and the statue of Shabbatil, waiting for his victims. When he came to the end, I said nothing. How Peter Lazenby must have exulted to come across a letter like this.

'There must have been . . .' I began.

At that moment, the door opened and Nicola came in. The moment I looked at her I knew that something was wrong. She'd been upstairs in our bedroom, writing up her diary.

'Tom, you've got to come quickly. It's Adam.'

'What's happened?' I was already out of my chair.

'I don't know. I heard some noises from his room, then he called out. I went there, but he can hardly get a word out. Didn't you hear anything?'

'It's too windy,' I said, dashing for the door.

Adam was huddled in a corner of his room, speechless, shaking with fear. At first he was all I could see. My whole attention focussed on him. I went up to him and bent down, holding his upper arms tightly in an attempt to stop his helpless shivering.

'What's wrong, Adam? It's Tom. Speak to me. Tell me what's wrong.'

He could not answer. He was talking now, but none of what he said made any sense.

'Is it Simon?' I demanded. 'Has he come back? Look at me, Adam, try to think. Tell me what you saw.'

A soft voice spoke behind me.

'Tom, I think you should look at this.'

It was Tim. He'd come up after me.

'Look,' he said.

I got to my feet and looked round the room. It was as though the storm outside had burst in and torn it apart. The walls had been stripped bare of everything: posters, pictures, a mirror, even wallpaper. Someone had scrawled long looping letters across the naked plaster. No, that is not correct. Not across, but through. The letters had been cut into the plaster, uncovering a darker layer underneath. They must have been incised with something very sharp. A nail, perhaps, or a knife. But another image came to me: a long talon.

I knew they were letters, that together they must form words; but try as I might, I could make no sense of them. Then, as though everything came together all at once, I realized that the words on the wall and the words Adam was repeating so indistinctly were one and the same. I did not know the chapter or the verse, but I knew the book: Revelations. The quotation ran all round the room like a black snake, a single verse written again and again, as though to chain us in:

Babylon is become the habitation of devils, and the hold of every foul spirit, and a cage of every unclean and hateful bird.

I looked at Andrew, then at Adam, still shaking in the corner. The wind rattled the window, straining to break through.

'What can have done that?' I asked. I thought of the cuts on Linda Turner's skin, of Addu of Sippar with his sacrificial knife.

'I don't know,' said Andrew. 'But one thing I do know. It's in Peter Lazenby's handwriting.'

Chapter Twenty-five

From P. R. Lazenby, 'Utukku and Etemmu in Old Babylonian Incantation and Exorcism Texts', Journal of Mesopotamian Religion (1953) 15 :237–49.

Fear of ghosts dominated the religious mind of Babylonians in this period. The dead dwelt in a drab underworld known as Aralu, whose rulers were the dark goddess Allatu or Erishkigal, 'the Mistress of the Great Place', and her consort Nergal, god of war and pestilence. With Nergal came all evil spirits and demons, above all the *utukku,* the seven evil ones.

More feared than these, however, were the restless ghosts of those who had remained unburied after death, or who had died in a state of disappointment, cheated of wealth or happiness during their lives. These spirits, the *ekimmu* or *etemmu* threatened the living, and among the priests a special class grew up whose task was to raise or exorcise or question the unhappy dead.

The fear remained, however. Above all, fear that the demon Shabbatil might one day have a son who would enter the underworld and bring forth the dead in such numbers that they would outnumber the living and take possession of the earth. The dead lived in dust, without light or water or pleasure of any kind, a wretched existence from which there could be no escape. No escape, that is, unless Shabbatil answered their prayers and sent his son to bring them back to the world of sunshine, where he would reign supreme.

Shabbatil, of course, is Satan in another guise. His winged and tailed image gave rise to a recurring iconography of the Devil in later art. To this day, however, the only representations we possess of this Great Demon are those on votive reliefs, and a detail from the seal of the cylinder belonging to the scribe Adda. Some textual evidence suggests that at least one statue of Shabbatil was located in Babylon, and that it was the object of a long-enduring devotional cult.

From the Journal of Peter Lazenby:

26 January 1963

The bell again last night. I wish it would give me peace. And the piping of that wretched flute. It kept me awake all night. The boy is in the house now, of course. I haven't seen him, but I know. He is the first, the original. Each time one dies, there is another. I don't know if I have the courage for him yet, or for any of this. Only the thought of what I may be, of what I may still become keeps me to it. Otherwise, I don't think I could bear any of it.

29 January

I saw something in the street this evening, between the corner and reaching the house. It was dark, and I had only the street lights to go by, but I thought I saw a man in a hood waiting near my front steps. Or was it a hood?

3 February

The smell runs through the house now. It is there in the mornings when I wake up, and at night when I go to bed. I slept with Jennifer last night, the little red-head with small breasts. Four months it took, but it was worth it, as I knew it would be. We made love at intervals, and slept, and woke, and made love again. She asked me what the spicy smell was, and I said it was something from the past, that the house had belonged to a spice merchant.

6 February

The hooded man again. He carries a staff like the one in Baghdad. I do not like the look of him, but what choice do I have? I left the front door open tonight. Now I have invited him in, the die is cast. Will I dream tonight?

Chapter Twenty-six

Andrew agreed to provide Nicola and Adam with beds for the night. There was no question of their staying in the house a minute longer. He rang his wife Jennifer and explained that I'd been taken ill and that Nicola couldn't cope on her own at short notice. Adam had calmed down by then, and we thought that he'd recover fully once he was out of the house. I called a cab and put Nicola and Adam inside, giving the address to the driver. They drove off into the wind and darkness. I thought I might never see them again.

'I'll stay with you,' Andrew said. 'It's not safe to be alone in the house tonight.'

'There's no need.'

'There's every need. Whatever wrote that inscription may still be there.'

Neither of us slept. We went from room to room, as though searching for something we dreaded to find. But apart from Adam's room, there was nothing out of the usual. We did what we could to cover up the writing. I didn't know what else to do. We couldn't continue to live in the house, but that meant finding somewhere else at short notice. The house would not just be hard to sell: I didn't see how my conscience would let me put it on the market in the first place. I began to think it would be better to burn it down.

When I opened my paper next morning, the mysterious illness story had reached the front page. Three of the victims had died following a fever, and the others were starting to show similar symptoms. Another fourteen cases of sudden blindness had been reported, all in the Bloomsbury area. This time the story made perfect sense to me. I thought there was little point in going to the authorities with what I knew.

The phone rang just as I was about to set out for work with Andrew.

'Tom? This is Terry Forbes. Listen, I wonder if you'd mind staying on after closing today.'

'Well, I'm not sure, Terry. Something's come up at home, and . . .'

'It's just that we've decided to put that statue on display, the one your friend Ed Monelli brought over. We had confirmation this morning from Chicago. They're willing for us to keep the statue on a permanent loan basis, in return for some pieces from our store. Seems a good arrangement. The public will love . . . what's the name of the god again?'

'Shabbatil,' I said.

'I need you to do a write-up on where he came from, who he is, anything that seems suitable. We've got a display case ready, and I think he can go in later this afternoon.'

'Terry, I don't think this is a good idea.'

'Why not? We might even get some photos in the press. Look, I won't keep you: the traffic's terrible this morning.'

I stared at the receiver. Terry had hung up.

'Something wrong?' Andrew was at the door, ready to leave. I explained what Terry had told me.

'Is there any way you can stop it?'

I shook my head.

'I'm not senior enough. They didn't even bother consulting me about the decision.'

'That's the museum these days. Everything's down to the administrators: we humble scholars come somewhere after the cleaners in the pecking order.'

'I don't like it, Andrew. The statue's the focus for all that's been happening. The god Shabbatil and the angel Lucifer are one and the same person. I think Peter Lazenby's original plan was to bring the statue here, to London. He had to find it first, and his blindness interfered with that. And then he heard that a new expedition had gone out to Baghdad. I don't know if his death was the result of an accident or deliberate, but it seems to have allowed him to point Caroline Monelli in the right direction. Once the statue was here Lazenby's own powers grew out of all proportion. People have already started dying. I think that once the statue is on display, the deaths will increase and spread out from Bloomsbury to the rest of London, and from there God knows where else.'

Andrew said nothing. We'd both seen and read and heard enough to make what might otherwise have seemed extraordinary perfectly believable.

'The problem is,' I said, 'how do we stop it?'

'What are we fighting here?' asked Andrew. 'Shabbatil or Lazenby?'

'Both, I think. But Lazenby's power comes from Shabbatil.'

'From Satan, you mean.'

I nodded.

'Yes, from Satan, if you prefer.'

'Could we destroy the statue?'

I thought about it.

'It could be done, yes. It would mean gaining access to the exhibits after closing time, but I think we could manage that between us. But I don't think it would achieve much. The statue is a focus, and it seems to be important for some reason, nevertheless, it isn't Satan himself, just a Babylonian depiction.'

'Let's talk about it later,' Andrew said, glancing at his watch. 'It's time we got moving.'

The postman was coming up the steps just as we came through the front door. He had a few letters and a small parcel. I took them absent-mindedly and stuck them in my overcoat pocket.

We set off, despondent, despairing of a situation that was fast moving outside our control. He was at work in the city already, blinding, striking down, instilling fear. We drove at a crawl through long queues of snarling traffic, past men and women trapped in their lives, along streets lined with the trivial and the gimcrack. I gazed out through my window as Andrew drove. There were beggars in doorways, and old men in shabby suits, young men tottering on the edge of madness, pale women with anxious children, coughing their way to school. The streets were ripe for plague, more suited to the dead than the living.

As we turned a corner into Woburn Place, we were forced into the nearside lane by a bus, bringing us to a halt. I looked at the pavement. A man in a black overcoat suddenly stopped, dropping his briefcase. He put his hands to his head, and I heard him scream above the roar of the traffic. People avoided him, dodging and swerving in their eagerness to be away from whatever madness had caused this outburst. I saw him pitch and stagger, then crash against a shop window and fall to the ground.

I opened the car door and jumped out, almost tripping on the kerb. The man was moaning now, and calling aloud for help.

I bent down and took one of his hands in mine.

'What's wrong?' I asked. 'What's happened?'

'Oh, God, help me,' he cried. 'I can't see. I can't see a bloody thing. It's gone dark, completely dark. You've got to help me.'

I stayed with him until an ambulance came. The paramedics had a frightened air.

'It's the second case this morning,' the driver said. 'God knows where this is going to end.'

Andrew had gone on to the museum. I walked the rest of the way, a short distance. When I arrived, I found the statue of Shabbatil waiting on a pallet outside the store, ready to be moved to the main display room.

'He gives you the shivers, doesn't he?' said Terry, coming up behind me.

'Yes,' I said. 'Yes, he does.'

'Chicago were very helpful. I've been in touch with the press. *The Times* are sending someone round this afternoon, the *Telegraph, Guardian,* and *Independent* are booked in for tomorrow. But the really good news is I've got one of the Sunday supplements interested. I'm beginning to think we could build a larger exhibit round this one find.'

'Are people that interested in Babylonia nowadays?'

'Good God, Tom, you're out of touch. Babylon's part of the Old Testament—Nebuchadnezzar, Belshazzar's Feast, *Mene, Mene, Tekel, Upharsin.* In the last century, that brought them in in hordes every time there was a new discovery.'

'But no one believes in the Bible any longer.'

'Come on, Tom, get real. Have you been in any bookshops recently? There are shelves full of the latest crank theory about the Ark of the Covenant or the Dead Sea Scrolls. It's big stuff.'

'And how does Shabbatil fit into that?' I looked sideways at the statue. I almost thought it was smiling.

'He's Lucifer. The Babylonian original, the start of the legend. All we have to do is plant the idea in the heads of a few journalists and Bob's your uncle. You'll have to do your bit, mind you. Play up that side of things. Legends about the fallen angel.'

I swallowed a mouthful of bitter saliva.

'You know that's academic nonsense, Terry.'

'What does the public care about that? Cost-effectiveness, building a customer base, bringing in the punters—that's what it's about. You don't have to lie, you just have to say the right things. Take your time. I'll pop back around three.'

He turned and walked away, already planning his next project. Just as he reached the corner, however, he paused, then turned back to me.

'Have you heard about Andrew Hutchins?' he asked.

My heart contracted.

'Andrew? We came in together. What's wrong?'

'It's that mystery illness. He was just coming through the door when he went blind. They've taken him off to hospital. It's horrible. He's the third member of staff in two days. Keep it to yourself—we don't want to spark off a panic.'

Chapter Twenty-seven

They had taken Andrew to the Middlesex, a few blocks away. I went there at once, and asked to see him, but they wouldn't let me through. A nurse told me to wait until the registrar was free. I was shown to a small room next to the intensive care unit. A woman sat opposite me, huddled in her seat, her head cradled in her hands. On the walls, Department of Health posters advised safe sex and the avoidance of cigarettes in pregnancy. Someone had scribbled 'Safe Sex Kills Joy' on the first poster. An ugly stain had transfigured one wall. I waited, eerily conscious of how time was passing. I hadn't even had time to take off my overcoat.

I remembered that I'd slipped my mail into my coat pocket on leaving the house. Now, with nothing to do but wait, I took it out. A couple of bills, a circular from the Museums Association, something for Nicola from the National Library for the Blind. The thin parcel was a padded bag postmarked Cambridge. I didn't recognize the handwriting. Stripping away a band of sellotape, I pulled the bag open.

Inside I found a letter in the same handwriting on thick cream-coloured paper. With it was an object wrapped in tissue paper. I unfolded the letter.

> *Dear Dr Alton,*
>
> *I'm sorry if I seemed rude when you and Dr Bird came to visit, but I'm sure you will understand that I try to do what I think is best for Nick. We were very much in love, and before his illness we'd planned to get married. I would still go ahead, but he's frightened. He thinks that, if we were to have children, they would turn out abnormal in some way. Perhaps if he gets really well he'll see that's nonsense.*
>
> *Unfortunately, your visit did him little good. He's been very agitated since then, and the doctor had to*

*visit him early this morning. He still has bad dreams.
I'm unwilling to blame you, but I must ask you not to
come again, and please ask Dr Bird and her colleagues
to stay away as well. He doesn't need reminders. I
think he has talent enough to be a passable potter, and
I know his life will be very different if he can put
archaeology completely behind him. That may seem
harsh to you—after all, you're part of that world—but I
sincerely believe it's the only hope Nick has of ever
living a normal life again.*

*He asked me to send this to you. It's been on his
mind for days. He says it was found in the chamber
where they dug out Shabtil (is that right?). He had
charge of it and found it in his luggage when he got
back to this country. You are to use it, he says. And he
says you are to dream. He wants to read my letter
before I send it, otherwise I would say none of this. At
least you may be able to restore it to its proper owners.*

*He woke last night from the middle of sleep and
said something to me, or to the darkness, as though it
was listening. 'The goat-headed child.' He repeated the
phrase several times. The farm next door keeps goats
for milk and cheese. In the past, Nick used to go there
happily to get provisions. Since his return, he will not
pass their gate. Is there a meaning in it, do you think?
Does the goat have significance in your ancient
mythology?*

*Yours sincerely,
Sarah Jones-Hornsby*

I picked up the little package and unwrapped the tissue paper. Inside
I found an object unlike anything I had seen before. It was like a tiny
table made of clay and enamelled in dark blue. The top was perfectly
square and covered with a cuneiform inscription. At each corner was
a smooth ball. Nick had inserted a note of his own, folded small,
perhaps to hide it from Sarah. I unfolded it.

*I found this in the chamber with the statue, and started
work on the translation shortly before I left. It carries
the names of Ishtar, Marduk, Shamash, and Ea, and in*

the centre the name of the goddess Erishkigal. The inscription round the edge starts something like this: 'She who is dark, she who is dark, Mother of Ninazu; she who is dark, whose gleaming shoulders are hidden by no garment.' That's Erishkigal, of course. After that there are a few words I can't read, then the following: 'Ask of her what you will, and she will answer. She listens at morning and at night, and her voice is never silent.' I think this was used for divination, for seeking answers from the goddess. I don't know how it was used, but perhaps you will. I wish you luck.

I weighed the little object in my hand, wondering what on earth I was supposed to do with it. There was no question in my mind of its authenticity, but I could not guess how it had been used.

At that moment, the door of the waiting room opened and a man in a white coat stepped in. He was carrying a sheaf of buff folders under one arm.

'Dr Alton? My name's Richardson. I'm the registrar looking after Mr Hutchins. I'd like to have a word if you don't mind.'

'How is Andrew? Can I see him?'

He shook his head. His manner was that of the competent professional, but it did not wholly convince. In his mid-thirties, he was lightly tanned and well-dressed; his skin was fragrant with expensive after-shave. The sort of man of whom I usually felt instinctively jealous. He looked as if he could tackle anything, as if it was in his power to face the most hideous diseases head on and conquer them. But that was just the act. Underneath, he was scared, and I could smell it as strongly as I smelled the Gucci fragrance.

'I'm sorry, sir, but your friend's being kept in isolation for the moment. We're doing all we can to reassure him, but he's not responding very well. He seems unusually upset.'

'He's just gone blind.'

'Yes, of course. But he's almost incoherent. He keeps talking about . . .'

He glanced round at the woman facing us. She had taken her hands from her face and lifted her head. Red-rimmed eyes stared out of bloodless features. Her mouth was tightly closed.

'Why don't you come to my office,' Richardson said. 'We can

talk more easily there.'

He led me along silent, rubber-floored corridors to a cubbyhole of a room lit by fluorescent lights. An empty goldfish bowl spoke of an earlier attempt to add a touch of individuality. On the windowsill, yellowing ferns wilted in the over-heated hospital atmosphere.

He closed the door and threw the files he'd been carrying to the floor before hurling himself onto one of the two chairs that fought for space with a desk and a filing cabinet. I took the other seat and glanced at him again. In here, he was able to let his guard down. I almost thought the tan faded from his face. He was face to face with a crisis that he knew could escalate within hours into his worst nightmare. There was nothing I could say that might reassure him. His worst nightmare was nothing compared to mine.

'We're worried,' he said. 'This could turn into a full-blown epidemic. At the moment it's confined to Bloomsbury, but it won't be long before we get cases outside the area. The problem is we just don't know enough about the individual cases to make even half-educated guesses about the possible cause. Was your colleague in contact with anything out of the ordinary in the past few weeks?'

'I really have no idea.'

'There've been several cases in the Museum. We're working on the assumption that it may be a possible source. Since it's a public building, any one of the victims may have paid a visit there in the recent past, but that's hard to establish. One man certainly did, apart from those who worked there.'

'There's nothing in the public areas that could . . .'

'We don't know that yet. At the moment we're trying to isolate the disease agent. The trouble is, we don't know what we're looking for. The illness doesn't follow any normal pattern. We are thinking of closing the museum, as a precaution. But we need authorization for that. You've no thoughts?'

'You said that Andrew kept talking about something.'

He ran his hand lightly through his hair, tousling it. At any other time, it might have looked boyish. Now it was the gesture of a tired man who doesn't know where to turn.

'He said something about the devil getting his revenge. Demons taking people's sight away. I'd say he was raving, but . . .'

He looked at me as if afraid I was about to accuse him of raving as well.

'But two of the other victims said something very similar. They'd go to sleep and wake an hour or two later saying they'd been dreaming of demons. Terrible beings with black wings.' He hesitated. 'I thought, perhaps . . . Is there anything in the museum that would correspond to that description?'

'Not on display,' I said.

'But there is something . . .'

'It goes on display this afternoon,' I said. I gave him what details I could. Perhaps I could at least prevent them putting the statue into its display case.

'Have you notified Andrew's wife?' I asked.

'I'm not sure. That's not my job; but I can find out.'

'If you would.'

He made a quick phone call. They hadn't got round to it yet.

'I'll do it,' I said. 'My wife's staying at their house anyway, along with my son. I'd like to check they're all right.'

I got up to leave. He came with me to the main entrance.

'I have to ask you to keep what I've told you to yourself,' he said as I was about to go. 'We daren't risk a mass panic. If the tabloids got hold of this thing about demons . . .'

'I've got better things to do than talk to the tabloids,' I said. I gave him a string of telephone numbers where I might be reached. 'Let me know if Andrew's fit to talk.'

'He'll be in isolation.'

'There's such a thing as a telephone.' I looked at him steadily. 'This is important,' I said. 'The minute he seems coherent, get in touch.'

I went back to my office. Everyone I passed seemed affected by the news about our colleagues. It now seemed the disease could strike any one of us in an instant. No one was safe, no one knew how to be safe. I heard an item on the eleven o'clock news. The outbreak was fast taking on the proportions of a national health scare. Four more victims had been reported: a child in a local school, a doctor, a policewoman from the station on Theobalds Road, and a lecturer at London University. It didn't say what he'd been a lecturer in. I wondered if it had been archaeology. A fifth man had been killed by a lorry while crossing the road in Russell Square. Witnesses said he'd started behaving strangely as he got halfway across, and it was suspected that he'd been struck by the disease at that very moment.

No one would comment further until the results of a post-mortem.

I picked up the phone to ring Jennifer, then changed my mind. I'd never met her, never even spoken to her. I punched in Terry's number.

'Terry, who on the staff knows Andrew well?'

'I'm not entirely sure. Paul Harrison should know. I'll give him a ring.'

I put the receiver down and switched on the radio again. A woman was talking about the Syakkei gardens of Kyoto. Her every other word was 'peace' or 'tranquillity'. I listened, waiting for the phone to ring. Suddenly, an announcer's voice broke in with a news flash.

'We're interrupting Hannah Fawcett's talk on Japanese horticulture to bring an update on the mysterious illness that has now acquired seventeen victims in London's Bloomsbury district. The name has just been released of one of this morning's victims. He is Dr Seán Brennan, a consultant at the Royal London Homoeopathic Hospital in Great Ormond Street.'

Chapter Twenty-eight

I went to Islington with a woman called Vivien. She had long dark hair streaked with grey, and huge, startled eyes that must have been her winning feature back in the Sixties, but now looked sad and frightened. She smoked thin brown cigarettes through a stubby holder. I'd seen her a few times before, in the canteen or passing in a corridor, laden with papers. She worked in Central Asian antiquities, and had been a close friend of Andrew's for something like twenty years.

No one had thought to venture in to her office to tell her about Andrew until Terry had rung through. I told her what I could on the way to the house. It was very little. I knew the truth, but what help would that have been? We sat side by side in a half-empty carriage on the tube, a little capsule of light swept through darkness. Vivien tried her best to make polite conversation, but it faltered, and in the end we travelled in silence.

Jennifer already knew. The hospital had finally acted independently and sent someone round to break the news. And then to say she should stay at home and only come in if asked. She was distraught by the time we got there. Nicola was doing her best, but she was a stranger.

We left Vivien with her, and I took Nicola to a room at the back. She hadn't heard about Seán.

'What's going on?' she asked. 'It's too much of a coincidence that two people we know are victims of this illness.'

I told her what I could.

'You've been keeping me out of this, Tom. But I can help, I know I can. Let me have Lazenby's papers. I'll go through them and see if I can spot something you've missed.'

'I don't have time to read them to you, love. I have to . . .'

'I'll scan them. Please. I need to be doing something.'

Her parents had bought her an audio scanner about a year earlier. Unlike a normal scanner, it didn't reproduce text, but provided a vocal rendering of what it read. The voice wasn't always smooth, and its vocabulary was limited, but it was still something of a miracle. The version used by Nicola allowed handwriting recognition as well.

'All right. I'll go through it this evening. A lot of it's in Arabic and Babylonian. I don't imagine the scanner will make much sense of that.'

She smiled.

'I just want to know about Lazenby. Give me what you can. In the meantime, I think I should call on Maeve. She doesn't really have anyone to help at a time like this.'

'I'll go with you,' I said. 'Then I have to go home. We still have to work out what we're doing about where we live. I think you should take Adam to your parents' for a week or two.'

'Adam can't afford to miss school. And I don't want you going back there. I'm afraid for you.'

'I'll be all right.' I put my hands on her shoulders. She struggled free.

'All right?' she retorted. 'After what's been happening?'

I took her again, more firmly this time.

'We have to see this thing through, Nicola. I won't let it beat me. Look, all I want to do is get a few things. Lazenby's papers, anything that may help. Have you thought of asking Maeve if you can stay at her place? You've said yourself she'll need someone. Adam can look after Michael.'

'What about you?'

'Well, maybe I can stay there as well. For a day or two at least, until we get this sorted out.'

'I don't know. She's . . . different. I've no idea how she'll cope with this. She may have relatives . . . I don't know.'

'We'll go over there now. Then I'll fetch your scanner and some of the papers.'

We went by cab. I dropped Nicola at the Brennans', then went on to our house. Nothing had changed. Entering alone, I felt the silence gather about me. Every movement, every tiny noise seemed an intrusion. Without Nicola and Adam, I felt myself a stranger in my own home.

I went to the kitchen and made myself a ham sandwich. The

fridge was full of food that might never be eaten now. The sandwich dropped like lead to my stomach, and I washed it down with cold beer. Normally, I didn't drink at lunch, but that day was not like any normal day.

The phone rang. I picked it up, swallowing a last mouthful of bread.

'Darling, it's Nicola. Are you all right?'

'I'm fine. I've been having a sandwich.'

'Maeve says you can stay here as long as you need. She's grateful for the company.'

'Does she understand how ill Seán is?'

'I . . . I'm not sure. They won't let her go to the hospital. There's been another item on the news. Two more victims, one of them in Hampstead. They're letting Michael come home from school. Could you pick him and Adam up, do you think?'

'Yes, all right.'

I went to Nicola's study and got the scanner and her lap-top. Leaving them in the car, I put together as much of Lazenby's stuff as I could. The phone rang again.

'Dr Alton? This is Dr Richardson. We met earlier at the hospital.'

'I remember.'

'Your friend Mr Hutchins is a little calmer now. He knows he can't have visitors at present. I spoke with him a little. He told me that an artefact had been brought back from Iraq, that it was now in the museum. He didn't give me any details. But apparently there were some deaths in a town called Hillar.'

'Hilla.'

'Do you know anything about this?'

'The deaths were from eating contaminated meat.'

'This artefact . . . Your friend seemed very worried about it. It couldn't be contaminated in some way?'

'Not in the way you mean, no.'

'Then in what way?'

'When I understand it myself, I'll let you know.'

'He said something else. It sounded important. He said I was to tell you.'

'Yes?'

'He says he saw Lazenby in the museum before he went blind. In a corridor near this artefact. Does that mean anything to you?'

I replaced the receiver. As I did so, a bell rang, tinny and indolent in the quiet air. I picked up a box of papers and carried it to the car.

It took me over an hour to do my errands. Michael was upset, Adam calmer than I had seen him. Whether in response to his friend's distress, or as a counter-reaction to his own agitation of the previous evening, he seemed detached, almost supercilious.

'What are you planning to do now?' Nicola asked when I handed over the papers and her equipment.

'I'm not sure. I won't go back to the museum today. I'll get some clothes and things for all of us, then lock the house up. Stay here with Maeve. I'll be back soon.'

She leaned forward and kissed me very gently on the lips.

'Take care,' she said.

I drove back through untroubled streets. A handful of people had been struck down by a mysterious virus in distant Bloomsbury. What did it matter in Islington or Hampstead or anywhere else? Good citizens went about their business, buying, selling, eating in restaurants with curtained and tinted and blinded windows. I tried to picture myself among them, and I could not.

I felt the sense of threat the moment I stepped back inside the house. All morning, thoughts had been churning inside my head without reaching any resolution. I was fighting a losing battle. Without Andrew Hutchins to offer advice, I felt lost and helpless.

I went back to the kitchen and took off my coat, draping it across a chair. As I did so, the package sent by Nick Parrish fell out onto the seat. I picked it up and unwrapped it, then set the little object on the table. It sat there, carrying its mute little inscriptions like heraldic mottoes on a shield. Nothing like it had ever been found in a Mesopotamian excavation before. I could not begin to guess its purpose. Idly, I reached out a finger and pushed it. It moved smoothly over the polished surface of the table. I pushed it the other way, and it shifted like a boat on the flat water of a lake. Like a child playing with a toy car, I rolled it back and forth, left and right, without thought or direction.

Suddenly I stopped dead. Perhaps this was how it had been intended to be used in the first place. I thought desperately. I knew a little about Babylonian divination, about the significance of names. Could there have been a board inscribed with the names of gods and goddesses, could a priest have moved the little enamel table across it, finding meaning in where it stopped? Could it have been the prototype of a modern ouija board?

I sat for a long time, thinking this over. I could feel the house watching me, could sense something moving within it. An inner voice warned me to leave, but I could not tear myself away from the little table.

I got up and went to the study, where I found a large sheet of white paper in a desk drawer. Taking it back to the kitchen, I wrote the letters of the alphabet and the numbers one to ten in a circle. I sellotaped the paper to the table, then took the little device and set it on top. I felt sure it would be a waste of time. Didn't it need more than one person to operate an ouija board anyway?

I rested my fingers lightly on top and pushed idly, left, right, up, down. Each time the device touched a letter, I dutifully wrote it down. Somewhere, the bell tinkled. Above me, the light flickered twice. I glanced at the letters I'd already written down: GKLOVBYTRMJJSAT . . . Gibberish, even in Babylonian. I tried again, trying to let the device move of its own accord. More gibberish. I tried spinning it, and almost sent it flying onto the floor.

Something was moving through the house. I wished I'd heeded Nicola's warning, and not come here alone after all. The little bell rang feverishly. I got up from the table and lifted my coat from the chair. I could feel it moving above me, in another room, but I could not say where. I put my coat on and made for the door. Something moved behind me.

I turned slowly. On the table, the enamel device was moving in a slow circle of its own volition. As I watched, it moved to the letter A, then to B, then to C, then to the centre of the circle, where it stopped. Like someone in a trance, I walked back to the chair and sat down.

Whatever had been moving through the house was no longer moving. It was here, with me in the kitchen. My mouth felt dry, as though I had eaten an unripe persimmon. I wanted to urinate. The air felt thick, not like air at all, but another substance. All across my skin, small spiders walked on the thinnest of legs, thousands of them, like a moving carpet. My tongue lay in my mouth like wax.

'Who . . . are you?' I asked out loud.

I couldn't take my eyes off the little blue table. It rocked for a moment, then shot to the letter L. Then A, Z, E, N, B, Y.

'Where are you?'

E, V, E, R, Y, W, H, E, R, E. The table flipped back to the centre of the paper, then started again. N, O, W, H, E, R, E.

'Are you here?' I asked. 'In this room.'

A, L, W, A, Y, S, W, I, T, H, Y, O, U.

'Can I see you?'

N, O, T, Y, E, T.

'Why not? Nick Parrish saw you in Babylon.'

H, E, W, A, S, R, E, A, D, Y. Y, O, U, A, R, E, N, O, T.

'Ready for what?'

T, H, E, B, L, I, N, D, W, I, L, L, S, E, E, A, N, D, T, H, E, D, E, A, F, W, I, L, L, H, E, A, R.

'I don't understand that.'

Y, O, U, W, I, L, L, U, N, D, E, R, S, T, A, N, D, S, O, O, N.

'Are you alone?'

The device seemed to hesitate. It moved a fraction, now in this direction, now in that, as if Lazenby could not make up his mind, or was uncertain of the answer. I, A, M, N, E, V, E, R, A, L, O, N, E.

'Who's with you?'

No hesitation now. T, H, E, D, E, A, D.

For a moment, I had the impression of a crowded room, a room packed with the pale faces of countless men and women. The next moment, both the faces and the faint impression of them in my mind's eye had faded. And then I saw, sitting in the chair opposite me, an old man with sunken cheeks and watery eyes. Not Peter Lazenby. My father. He looked at me as if he was looking at a stranger. Then he too faded, and I was left staring at a circle of letters and figures, at a little enamelled device, at an empty room.

'Are you still there?' I asked tentatively.

There was no movement. No sound. Not even a breath of air. But there was still something in the kitchen. I moved back my chair and stood.

'Who's there?' I asked. 'Are you still there, Lazenby?'

Nothing moved.

'Then who is there?'

Very slowly, the thing on the table moved. I watched it, feeling more frightened than ever. There were spiders on my skin again. Web after web, leg upon leg, crawling.

S.

I watched it creep round the circle.

H.

I backed away slowly from the table.

A.

I started moving towards the door.

B.

I put my hand on the door handle.

B.

I ran out. When I reached the street, it was dark outside, and very, very cold.

Chapter Twenty-nine

My father had taken more than a year to die. It had not been an easy departure. Every day of his illness, he'd asked for death, and every day, till the very last, he'd been denied it. He wanted peace, nothing more; and he'd consoled himself—as we'd all consoled ourselves—by thinking of death as just that. Oblivion, or an eternal sleep in which no pain could ever come to him again. But that afternoon he'd sat facing me with a look in his eyes that spoke of greater pain than any he had suffered on this earth. I could not easily rid myself of the image, or the thoughts it inspired.

By the time I got to Maeve's, my thoughts had cleared a little. The house was full of women from her church, and a couple of nuns who clucked like hens as they went about their task of consolation. Seán was not dead, but nobody seemed to think he was getting any better. I didn't blame them.

Nicola was waiting patiently for the hubbub to subside. 'She'll want to talk to me,' she said, 'when this is over.'

In a little room on the ground floor that Maeve had set aside as a place for the family's devotions, a group of women prayed before an image of the Virgin. The smell of incense filled the house, frankincense, galbanum, sandalwood, and myrrh. The soft voices of women praying mingled with Maeve's sobbing. A little bell rang constantly, unsettling me without reason. The priest was due later.

Nicola had started work on the scanning. Some of Lazenby's journals had been typewritten, and she'd started with these. A cold, uninflected voice read back to her the details of bizarre thoughts and ugly memories. I left her to it, thinking she was safe.

'The baby's twice as big as it was,' she said as I was leaving. 'It won't be long now.'

I looked at her. She was right. He was not prepared to wait much longer.

I drove to Kensington, to the address I had for the Iranian magician, Ali Baba. With Andrew incapacitated, I needed help, and I couldn't think where else to find it.

He lived in a basement underneath a Persian restaurant called the Tah-Dik. There were photographs in its windows of cabaret artists— refugees from Las Vegas or Hollywood posed before huge microphones, singers with glossy lips, musicians performing on the *nay* or the *santur*. Ali Baba appeared on Saturday evenings. His photograph had faded, and one corner had peeled away from its backing.

His name was on the bell, in Roman and Persian script. I pressed the button and waited. A young woman answered the door. She was very beautiful, like a miniature come to life. Something about her seemed familiar. I guessed she must be Ali Baba's daughter.

'Dr Alton? Why don't you come in,' she said. 'He's expecting you.'

'But that's impossible. He doesn't know . . .'

'He's been waiting for you since this morning. Please, come in.'

She went ahead of me down a long corridor lined with intricate calligraphy. I realized where I'd seen her before: she was one of the singers from the restaurant.

He was waiting in a back room, dressed in a plain black suit. Albert Einstein, Coco the Clown, Albertus Magnus. All the theatricality had gone. This was the real man.

'Thank you, Mahvash,' he said.

She showed me to a chair beside a low table inlaid with mother-of-pearl. On it sat a huge bowl filled to the brim with salted pistachios. Mahvash smiled at me as she left, but I detected a trace of anxiety in her eyes.

As the door closed, he looked at me and sighed.

'*Agar an Turk-e Shirazi be-dast arad del-e ma-ra*
Be-khal-e Henduyash bakhsham Samarqand u Bukhara-ra.'

I looked back at him blankly and his face opened in a soft smile.

'Hafiz,' he said. 'Do you English not know of him now? Or is Omar Khayyam still the extent of your knowledge, *Aqa*?'

'I know the name.'

He nodded glumly.

'And you are an educated man. What hope is there? Your Sir William Jones translated those lines very beautifully:

"Sweet maid, if thou would'st charm my sight,
And bid these arms thy neck infold;
That rosy cheek, that lily hand,
Would give thy poet more delight
Than all Bocara's vaunted gold,
Than all the gems of Samarcand." '

He sighed again. 'It's rather free,' he said, 'but it has the spirit.'

'She's very beautiful,' I said. 'Is she your daughter?'

'Mahvash? Yes. *Khayli qashang e.* She's studying English at Westminster University. Perhaps one day she will make a new translation of Hafiz.'

'She said you were expecting me.'

He hesitated. On the wall above him hung a photograph of a family group. Judging by his appearance, it had been taken ten or more years earlier. Was the woman by his side his wife, I wondered, or a sister perhaps?

'Yes,' he said. 'I've been waiting for the past few days. I knew you would enter my life again, *Jinab.*'

'Can you help me?'

He hesitated again.

'I don't know. *Shayad.* Perhaps. I need to know more. At the moment all I know is that you are very frightened. If it's any use, I will tell you that I am frightened too. What I saw that day in your house was no ordinary evil.'

It took a long time to go through it all with him. He interrupted me frequently, asking questions that would not have occurred to me. His manner was solemn, and grew more solemn as I continued. It was early evening by the time I finished. He asked if I would eat with him.

'I'm not very hungry,' I said. I realized that I'd been eating less and less over the past few days.

'Nevertheless, you must eat, *Aqa.* We will both need our strength tonight and tomorrow. Enough time has been wasted already. We have to go back to your house tonight. The centre of the evil is there.'

'Then you are willing to help?'

'What choice do I have, *Jinab?* None of us is safe, none of us can hide from this. Mahvash has cooked Abgusht—it's a Persian stew, you'll find it quite delicious. Don't worry, there'll be enough for all of us. After all, *Aqa,* I was expecting you.'

Mahvash ate with us, and during the meal we kept off the topic that had brought me there. We talked of literature and theatre and the mullas in Iran. But my mind gave me no relief. All through the meal, I felt as though a glass screen was keeping me apart from the real world. On one side of the screen I could see a beautiful young woman, talking about poetry and music and a distant country where nightingales sang beneath the full moon. On the other side—the side I inhabited—everything appeared misshapen and desperately forlorn.

At the end of the meal, when Mahvash had cleared the table and gone to her room to work, Ali Baba turned to me.

'You should know my real name,' he said. 'I am Bahram. Bahram Safa'i'

He paused and put a piece of Persian candy in his mouth.

'I've been thinking,' he went on. 'This woman who had sex with Lazenby and perhaps with . . . this other thing.'

'Linda.'

'Yes. Why did she make it public?'

'I'm not sure. She didn't say.'

'You say there were a lot of women. What happened to them all?'

'Again, I don't know.'

'I think you should ring this Linda. I think you should ask her about the object they wore round their necks.'

'You mean in the photographs?'

'Yes. In the photographs, *Aqa.*'

'You think that's important?'

He looked at me like a sad-eyed dog. A spaniel or a pug. He was older than he looked. A refugee who has lost all hope of restoration.

'There is something about it that I do not like. Call it a hunch. I want to know about this before we go back to your house. Do you have her telephone number here?'

It was in my diary. I looked it up and he showed me to a telephone hidden behind a framed photograph of a woman in her late thirties or forties.

'Your wife?' I asked.

He nodded. His face seemed to lose all its animation.

'Shirin died two years ago,' he said. 'Very suddenly. A car accident. *Khoda rahmatash kunad.* Please, you should ring Miss Turner. Ask her about the pendants.'

The phone rang five or six times before she answered.

'Linda? This is Tom Alton.'

A hesitation as she gathered her courage.

'Yes, Tom. What can I do for you?'

'Can I ask you some more questions? Not many. It won't take long.'

I heard her sigh on the other end.

'Now? I was . . .'

'I don't have to come over. It's important.'

'Yes, I know. I understand that. What do you want to know?'

I hesitated. There was no delicate way of putting any of this.

'What made you go to the authorities? Was it revenge, or did someone else suggest it?'

There was a long silence. I could hear a whistling sound on the line, very faint, as though the connection passed through a long, uncharted wilderness.

'Something . . . unpleasant happened.,' she began. 'Beyond what I've already told you. He . . . The fact is, I told him I was pregnant. I'd missed my period, and I was worried. Back then . . . well, I thought my parents would kill me. Peter was the only person who could look after me. I didn't think . . . I didn't expect him to marry me or anything. Just that he'd see I was all right. Or maybe arrange an abortion. I don't know, I was too worried at the time to think straight.

'I thought he'd be angry, annoyed with me for complicating things; but he wasn't—he was delighted, over the moon. He . . . that night he . . . gave me something that he said was very special. A gold disc with a chain on it. It was some sort of talisman, with what he said was Babylonian writing on it. He said it was a special present to celebrate the fact I was expecting a baby. I was supposed to wear it all the time from then on. He . . . took photographs of me wearing it.'

'In the nude?'

'Yes . . . Please, I'm not finding this easy. But, yes, I was naked. I don't know what he did with the photographs. Perhaps he kept them. Perhaps you've already seen them. You said you had his things.'

I said nothing, and in a moment she went on.

'Things stayed like that for about a fortnight. I was happier than I'd ever been in my life. I did start thinking we might get married then. Every day I thought about what we'd do when we were husband and wife. It felt terribly grand at that age to think I'd become a lecturer's wife. It meant something in those days. Not like now.'

'What happened after that?'

Another pause.

'I . . . My period came. A heavy one. I hadn't been pregnant, it had all been a fantasy.'

'You hadn't been to a doctor?'

'No, I'd just assumed . . . Anyway, I told Peter that night and . . . I've never seen anyone change the way he did. He got so angry I was really terrified. I thought he was going to kill me or something. He threw me out of the house. I broke my arm. That was when I decided to go to the university authorities. The rest . . . Well, you know what happened.'

'What about the talisman? The gold disc.'

'Oh, Peter took that back. He tore it from my neck. It hurt for days afterwards. I can still feel it burning on my skin sometimes. Even now.'

'Did you know there were other women he gave that talisman to? Or ones like it—there might have been more than just one.'

'No. I knew about the other women, but not about the talisman.'

Her voice sounded very small and hurt. On the line, voices that were not voices whispered. I thought I could hear the ghost of a wooden flute being played in the darkness between Linda and myself.

'It doesn't matter, Linda. You did the right thing to expose him.'

'The right thing? From whose point of view? It finished me. I'd keep quiet if I had the chance again. If he'd taken me back, I'd have gone to him.'

'These other women,' I pressed on, 'did you ever meet any of them?'

'No. I tried to, of course, but . . . the university wanted it all hushed up as quickly as possible. I wasn't encouraged to get in touch with them. I can't even remember their names now. But no doubt they're on file somewhere.'

'Yes. Yes, I'm sure they are. Thank you for telling me all this. You've been very brave.'

'I'll be here if you need me,' she said. 'Take care.'

She hung up. I was left with silence and music that was not quite music.

I put down the receiver and turned to Bahram. I told him what Linda had told me. When I finished, he looked at me gravely.

'It's time to go,' he said.

Chapter Thirty

I drove. Bahram sat beside me, playing with a string of amber worry-beads. His fingers moved like a seamstress's, knitting patterns and discarding them.

'I come from a little place called Shiraz,' he said. 'Have you heard of it, *Aqa*? The city of roses and nightingales. Hafiz the golden-tongued is buried there. And Sa'di, who wrote the poem of the Rose Garden. I used to visit their tombs with a group of school friends. We'd drink a little wine and read some poetry. After a few hours, the sun would go down, and in minutes the sky would fill with stars, and before long the moon would come up above our heads like a lamp. We always timed our visits so there would be a moon. In summer, there were always clear skies.'

I was stuck behind a bus, but made no attempt to pull out and pass it. The longer it took to get to where we were going, the happier I would be.

'When I first arrived in London, *Aqa*,' Bahram continued, 'I was overwhelmed. I had never seen such a place as this, not even that great city Tehran. All these vain streets, all these bright shops, all these stone-built houses. It seemed almost magical, do you know—a city of the jinn, something built by Solomon.'

I remembered the drab pavements and broken-down doorways I'd seen that morning. Now, in the dark, a little magic had returned. If I hadn't known what else lay behind the façade of darkness and lights, I might have been deceived.

Bahram took a crumpled cigarette from his pocket and lit it with the lighter from the dashboard. A warm smell of hashish filled the interior. He inhaled deeply several times, then made to pass the reefer to me.

'No, thanks,' I said. 'I need to keep my mind clear.'

He went on smoking, saying nothing, and gazing through the

windscreen. I wondered what he really saw.

'He gave them all talismans,' he said at last. His voice and his manner had changed abruptly. 'Ten, twenty, thirty—who knows how many? The talisman was a token of their importance. They were pregnant, they were carrying his children.' He hesitated. 'Or perhaps not his children.'

I shuddered, thinking of the thing in the drawing Linda had given me. And I thought too of what might be coming alive in Nicola's womb. It was growing impatient.

'What happened to them after that?' I asked.

He stubbed out his cigarette in the ashtray, slowly, as if savouring the act. The sweet smell still lingered. I couldn't help breathing it in. It made me a little light-headed. In the street in front of me, lights danced like will-o'-the-wisps.

'I think he killed them. I'm not sure why. But I have a strong feeling about it.'

'Are you really a magician?'

'You mean, do I have powers above the natural? Yes. My father was a magician, and his father, Fakhr Ali Shah.'

'He was a king?'

'No, a Sufi. A dervish. But also a magician. I have inherited some of his powers. I can see things that other men do not see. I saw things in your house that I wish I had not seen.'

'And you think Lazenby killed these women? Surely that makes no sense. If they were carrying his child, or Shabbatil's.'

'Nevertheless, it is what I feel. Have you a garden?'

I was forced to pass the bus. We were nearly in Hampstead.

'Yes, a small one,' I said. I felt a shudder pass through me.

'A cellar?'

'Yes.'

'I think we should go to the cellar first.'

We arrived fifteen minutes later. The house was dark. I had left no lights on. I found a parking space a few yards away, slotted the car in, and switched off the engine. A profound silence washed across us. Nothing was moving in the street. No cars, no bicycles, no pedestrians. It seemed deserted.

My hand shook as I slipped the key into the lock. I didn't want to go back in there. I switched on the hall light. Nothing had changed. But I could smell it right away, a scent of spices. And something else this time, familiar yet unidentifiable.

I led Bahram down to the cellar. The smell of spices gave way to a musty smell. But that other, unidentifiable smell remained, just present, like a memory that snags the brain but will not make itself fully known.

We hadn't done much to the cellar since moving in. I'd put up a small wine rack and bought bottles from time to time to go in it. Other odds and ends littered it: a broken bicycle, a stack of flower pots that I'd been meaning to put bulbs in, Nicola's old Braille typewriter, cans of paint, a pair of stilts Adam had given up using, a discarded record player with an LP still on the turntable.

Bahram walked to the centre of the room and stood with his eyes closed and his arms folded across his body. He remained like that for several minutes. Watching him, I felt something gathering in the air round us. The only illumination came from a naked light bulb in the ceiling above Bahram's head. He whispered to himself, words I did not and could not understand.

Finally, he opened his eyes. For a moment I think he did not recognize me or know quite where he was.

'It is here,' he said. 'Beneath the floor. Not deep.'

'Bodies? You're sure . . .?'

He had turned ashen. A light sweat peppered his forehead. Closing his eyes briefly, he shook his head.

'I am not sure. There is something here. Death. A great deal of death. There is no mistaking that. But something else. I am not frightened of some bones. But this . . . other thing frightens me very much. Nevertheless, we have no choice. We must dig.'

The light bulb flickered once. I hadn't thought to bring a torch. The thought of being trapped down here in pitch darkness was repellent. I looked at the floor. It was flagged with heavy stone slabs set tightly together. I wondered how hard it might be to dislodge them.

'We'll have to get these up,' I said. 'I'll fetch some tools. Will you be all right here on your own?'

He nodded, and I went up the steps back to the hall. The first thing that struck me was that it had grown very cold. I swore. Coming in from the cold, I hadn't noticed it before. The central heating should have been on.

I went to the kitchen, shivering. The heating controls were in a cupboard next to the sink. I opened it: the heating was running at its maximum setting. Stepping across to the nearest radiator, I put my hand on it: it was piping hot. But the room was freezing, and getting colder by the minute, or so it seemed.

I went out through the back door to the garden shed, where I found a torch and a variety of tools—a crowbar, a couple of spades, and a garden fork. I slipped the torch into my pocket and bundled the rest together in my arms. It was only as I was stepping back inside the house that I remembered none of the tools belonged to me. They had been Lazenby's. If he'd dug up the cellar, it had been with these.

It was colder than ever. My breath hung limp on the still air. Upstairs, someone was singing. It was a boy's voice, high-pitched, but tuneful. I knew it was Simon Passmore. He'd be looking for his friend Adam, I thought.

Back in the cellar, I explained to Bahram what had happened about the heating.

'It's what I would expect,' he said. 'The temperature will drop even further. Try to ignore it. If we dig hard, *Aqa*, it will keep us warm.'

He used the crowbar to dislodge the first slab. It wouldn't fit into the gap at first, and it took a lot of heavy blows to crack the stone sufficiently to make a hole. After that, it was a matter of brute strength. Half an hour later, we lifted the slab away to reveal a flat bed of compacted earth beneath.

I leaned the slab against one wall. When I turned back, Bahram was standing still in the middle of the floor.

'Who is the boy?' he asked.

I thought he meant Simon.

He shook his head.

'Not the one singing. The other one. He walked across the floor just now.'

'I saw no one.'

'Not to see. He wore a white robe. An Arab boy. He had a flute in his hand.'

'I think . . .'

I looked down at the patch of earth that had been uncovered. There was the unmistakeable imprint of a naked foot in its centre.

'I think we should hurry,' said Bahram. 'I'm frightened of this place. We are disturbing something that should not be disturbed.'

Now the first slab had been removed, it was easier work to lift several more. We cleared a wide area in the centre of the cellar and started to dig, side by side, piling up soil behind us. The smell that I had become aware of on entering the house grew stronger. It did not seem to come from the soil, but to be centred in it somehow. I bent and lifted a lump of it, smelling it, but I could not identify it. Perhaps it could be examined later. I wrapped the clod in my handkerchief and slipped it into my pocket.

We'd only gone down about three feet when Bahram's spade struck something solid. I swallowed hard. It helped if I pretended that I was on a dig, and that anything I might find had been here centuries. I looked down. Bahram was bending down and clearing a veil of soil away from a human skull. Some further digging revealed the beginnings of a complete skeleton.

'Keep digging,' he said. 'This is not all.'

I went on scooping up the chalky, half-damp soil around the remains we had uncovered. Moments later, my spade hit something. I knelt and began to lift the soil with my hands. This was not bone, but a bundle wrapped in cloth. I managed to get it free, and lifted it to the paving stones behind me.

It was about two feet in length, like a small mummy.

'Unwrap it,' Bahram said.

'Do we have to?' I'd already guessed what was inside.

He nodded. His face was very serious.

'I do not think it will be what it appears,' he said.

I found a pair of garden shears in a box and started to cut open the bundle. I felt dizzy, and I wanted to throw up. A terrible revulsion swept over me.

'Open it,' Bahram said. His voice was implacable. All trace of Coco the Clown had gone. His face was like stone.

I cut the bundle right down the centre, vertically, then pulled back the frayed layers of cloth. It had not decayed completely. A baby's arms and legs, a shrivelled torso. And then I looked at the head.

I think I nearly fainted then, and would have done so had Bahram not caught hold of me.

'Are you all right?' he asked. He'd seen it too. His skin was paler than ever.

'Yes. Yes, I'm all right.'

We looked down together at the pathetic little bundle I had

unwrapped. A baby's legs and arms, a desiccated torso—and the head of a goat, with the stumps of small horns.

I don't know how long it took us to uncover the rest. I lost all sense of time. Nor can I be sure we uncovered all of them, for I had no knowing of how far down Lazenby had dug. Eight women and eight babies. The women all wore gold discs round their necks, the babies all had the heads of goats.

I'm not sure when we first became aware of the flies. There was one to begin with, buzzing back and forth among the remains. Then three or four. As we dug down further, more appeared, until we could not ignore them. It was as if they were being generated from the bones or from the soil itself. A black cloud of them danced and tumbled through the cellar.

'We have to stop,' I said. 'This is pointless. What does it prove?'

'I think you know what it proves. These are his failures. But he will not always fail.'

At that moment, I heard a scratching sound, just audible above the humming of the flies. I looked up. On the wall facing me, a great tear had appeared in the plaster. As I watched, it started to form letters, then words.

Go now to the flock, and fetch me from thence two good kids of the goats; and I will make them savoury meat for thy father, such as he loveth.

No sooner had the letters formed than swarms of flies started to crawl over them, like a moving carpet.

'What does it mean?' asked Bahram.

'It's from the Bible,' I said. 'The Book of Genesis.'

I saw him then. The figure that had followed Lazenby through the streets of old Baghdad, dark, in a dark hood. He was standing in one corner of the low-ceilinged room, stooped over, a staff in his hand.

'Leave,' whispered Bahram sharply.

'We're going together.'

'No.' He turned to me, pleading. 'You have to leave. You have to go to your wife. Please, there's no time to argue. Let me deal with this. I can hold him long enough. But if you wait . . .'

He pushed me towards the door. I dropped the spade that had been in my hand. The figure in the corner was moving towards us. I could not make out its face. Perhaps it had none. Perhaps it had a thousand faces.

'Leave!'

I stumbled towards the stairs. In my ears, the buzzing of flies grew unbearable. When I looked back, they had formed like a curtain between me and Bahram. I hesitated only moments longer, then staggered up the stairs and into the hall and an odour of spices.

Chapter Thirty-one

I felt him beside me all the way back to Maeve's house, a small man with long hair and a moustache, urging me to hurry. I was still in a state of shock, far too preoccupied even to shed a tear for him.

As I turned the corner into Maeve's road, the first thing that caught my eye was a police car, parked outside the house. Had Seán already died? I parked opposite and stepped out, my heart pounding.

A policewoman answered the door. She let me in once I'd explained who I was, and took me through to the hall. The nuns and the other women had flown back to their roost, but from the little shrine room the voice of the priest could be heard, intoning prayers.

'You're wife's in the living-room with Mrs Brennan, sir,' said the policewoman.

'What's wrong? Why are you here?'

'The boys have gone missing, your son and Mrs Brennan's. We have officers looking for them. I understand this isn't the first time your son has gone missing, Dr Alton.'

'It has happened before, but not like this. Can I see my wife, please?'

'Yes, of course.'

Nicola and Maeve Brennan were sitting side by side on the sofa, holding hands, while Nicola spoke in a flat voice to a policeman, who was taking notes. I went up to her and kissed her on the forehead. I could see she'd been crying.

'Michael was very upset about his father,' Maeve said. 'I think he was more upset when he came home and found us all praying. A lot of hysterical Catholic women. I find them a little tiresome myself. We think he persuaded Adam to go off with him somewhere.'

'Have you tried the hospital where Seán's being kept?'

'It was the first place we thought of, sir.' The policeman was polite, but wary. He knew about the illness, knew he was in a house where someone had contracted it. It unnerved him, and it must have made it worse to be talking with a blind woman in a house where Catholic prayers formed a steady background hum. He was a thin Glaswegian with tight Presbyterian lips and hard, suspicious eyes.

'I need to talk to you, Tom.' Nicola got to her feet, letting go of Maeve's hand.

'I'm sure he'll be all right, dear. They'll have gone to see Seán. That's where they'll turn up.'

She shook her head. For the first time since I'd known her, I sensed frustration at her blindness.

'It's not about Adam. Can we . . .' She turned to the policeman. 'Officer, can I go upstairs with my husband? There's something we need to talk about in private.'

He scuttled to his feet.

'You don't have to ask my permission, Mrs Alton. You're free to do as you please in your own house . . . Or your friend's house. We've just finished here, anyway. If you don't mind, we'll get back to the station. We'll be in touch the minute there's anything to report.'

Nicola excused herself to Maeve and we went upstairs to the guest room.

'What's the matter,' I asked, 'if it isn't Adam?'

I heard the front door close.

'I couldn't tell you in front of them. They'd think . . .' She stopped in mid-speech and fell into my arms, weeping, clinging to me, kissing me. I held her to me, kissing her back, feeling a tremendous need for her after the horror I had just witnessed; but she pulled away, shaking her head and clutching her belly.

'This thing . . .' she moaned, 'this thing . . .'

'It's all right,' I said. 'It can't harm us.'

I knew I could not tell her what I had found in Lazenby's cellar. Instead, I tried to comfort her, stroking her hair and calming her as best I could. She recovered herself slowly.

'Here,' she said. 'I want you to hear this.'

She led me to the scanner, which she'd set up on the dressing table. From the box of papers that I'd given her, she took a single sheet and placed it face downwards on the plate. I watched her press the 'Scan' button. Her hands fell to her sides. We waited as the machine scanned and re-scanned the sheet.

Suddenly, out of the little speaker came a voice. Not the bland monotone of the machine, but a man's voice, fully inflected, speaking in the languorous accents of the old English middle classes. I did not doubt whose voice it was. Not for a moment.

'*September fourth*

'*Today recited the* Oracles of *Julian the Chaldaean, seven times, each hour on the hour. Then made love to the little French girl, vigorously, for above an hour. It hurt me to do what I had to do then, she was so pretty and I had so much pleasure of her. I think I even loved her a little. There was a lot of blood, I must be careful of that next time. She only cried out once.*

'*But all is well. He appeared to me as I left the room, and I knew I had pleased him. I tremble to think what I may yet become.*'

'It is his voice, isn't it?' Nicola asked.

'I don't know. Very likely.'

'It's the same voice I heard that day on the radio, and later in my dreams. What did he do to them? The women he slept with.'

'I'm not sure, he . . .'

'He killed them, didn't he?'

'Not all of them, that's inconceivable. But some of them, yes.'

'What did you find?'

'Some skeletons. We gave up in the end.'

'I've been sitting here for hours listening to . . . that. It has no right to be there.'

She reached out again for the box, and before I could stop her she had placed another document on the plate. Not a page from Lazenby's journal this time, but something else. A transcription of a Babylonian text. The computer scanned it through. There was a brief whirring noise, then another voice. Not Lazenby's voice. This was much more guttural, much more disturbing.

'*Lish-sha-kin-ma a-na nishemesh asaku*

Remu arhush lu kushurma ia u-she-sher sher-ra.'

Line after line it continued, a horrid, jarring incantation, in a voice that must have been dead long centuries. I do not know how long we stood there, transfixed by it, like frightened rabbits caught in the headlights of an articulated lorry.

The spell was broken by a cry from downstairs. I ran through the door to the top of the stairs.

Maeve was standing in the hall, holding her head in both hands and screaming. Beside her stood the priest, an old man in a black suit. He was outwardly calm, but his expression betrayed an agitation that he had to struggle to control.

'What happened? Has there been news?'

Maeve went on screaming. The priest looked at me.

'The prayer room,' he said. 'Go there and see for yourself.'

I hurried along the corridor with the sound of Maeve's cries ringing in my ears. The door to the room had been left wide open. All the lights were on. Against one wall stood a painted statue of the Virgin holding the infant Jesus. From the other walls, religious prints looked down. Every free surface was covered with candles; incense burned in front of the statue.

But I scarcely noticed any of that. What drew my attention were the flies. Huge black flies, monstrous and without number. Their buzzing filled the room. Some had fallen onto the naked flames of candles, and lay half burnt on the floor. Even as I watched, cloud upon blasphemous cloud descended on the statue, turning it black.

I left the room, sickened and repelled. Maeve was still shaking and crying. She had taken the incursion as an ill omen and thought Seán already dead. Perhaps he was, I didn't know. I made to comfort her, but as I did so I heard a sound on the stairs. I looked up. Nicola was standing there, one hand balanced on the banister.

'It's started,' she said. 'The baby. He wants to be born.'

Chapter Thirty-two

I rang for the midwife, and then I rang the hospital. Seán was still alive. Maeve calmed down and took Nicola upstairs to get her ready for the midwife's arrival. The priest, whose name was Shanks, was a dry stick of a man who had seen out five popes and seemed set to outlive the reigning one. I took him to one side.

'Father,' I said, 'I won't try to explain what is happening here tonight. You've seen a little for yourself. There is a very great evil at large. I want you to pray for my wife. Can you do that? She's not a Catholic, but she needs your prayers. Are you willing to stay with her throughout the birth?'

He seemed reluctant, knowing nothing of any of it, but in the end he nodded and said he would remain with her.

'There's something I have to do,' I said. 'It means leaving the house. I trust you to look after Nicola for me.'

'Shouldn't you be with her at a time like this?'

'Yes, I should. But if I don't do this thing a much greater evil will happen.'

I took him upstairs to the guest room. Nicola had already changed into one of Maeve's nightdresses and was being settled on the bed by her. I went to her.

'Darling, I can't stay with you. I've been thinking about what happened up here just now, and I think I know a way of stopping him. You'll have to trust me. Father Shanks will stay with you. I've asked him to pray for your protection.'

'Don't leave me, Tom. I'm frightened. I don't know what will happen.'

I sat on the edge of the bed and took her hand in mine. She was soaking with sweat. I put my free hand on her forehead and stroked it gently, pushing her hair back from her eyes. They were wide open, as if she was straining to see.

'I have to go, my love. If there were time, I'd stay with you. But time is the one thing we don't have. What happens tonight will decide all things for good or evil. I'll be back, I promise.'

I bent my head and kissed her on the lips. When I took my lips away, it felt as though I was parting from her forever.

I took the scanner with me and went outside to my car.

The house had not changed since I left it. All the way over, I had thought it possible. I did not know what we had unleashed, or what stage it had now reached. But anyone passing would have treated it as no more than a tall Georgian house in an unexceptional street, no different than its neighbours, in need of a little paint, nothing more.

I began to wish I'd asked Shanks to come with me. If nothing else, his prayers might have given me a little comfort. The door swung open on an empty hallway. The light was burning just as I had left it.

'Bahram? Bahram, are you there?'

There was no reply. I stepped inside, carrying the scanner with both hands, and kicked the door shut behind me. The house had grown warm since I left it. I went to the cellar door. It was still open.

'Bahram! Are you down there?'

I knew it was futile, but I had to try. Nothing would induce me to go back down those stairs. I called his name several times more, but he did not answer, and in the end I closed the door.

The house seemed to be holding its breath. I felt it watching me, following my every movement, holding me in its maw like a cat with a frightened mouse. I climbed the stairs slowly to the first floor landing. It was colder up here. Much colder. The door to the study was lying open. I could not remember whether or not I had left it like that.

I went inside and laid the scanner on my desk, making room for it by pushing papers and books to the floor. They crashed into the silence, and I immediately regretted letting them fall so loudly. I waited until the last echoes had faded away, then plugged the scanner in to the nearest socket and switched it on.

As it warmed up, I went to the shelves and began to pull out books and journals. I knew what I was looking for, but in my nervousness, my fingers fumbled and my memory went blank. But one by one I found them: Babylonian exorcism texts, prayers and incantations against the darkness that had not been read aloud in over two millennia.

As I put the last one on the little heap I was making, I heard a sound behind me at the door. I turned. Bahram was standing there, calmly watching me.

'Bahram? Thank God you're all right. I thought . . .'

He smiled.

'Can I come in?' he asked.

I was about to say 'yes' when I smelt the odour of spices.

'Who are you?' I asked.

'Bahram.'

'Bahram is dead. You've taken his image. Tell me who you are.'

'My name is Bahram. Bahram Safa'i. Let me in.'

I turned, lifting the top book of the heap and placing it on the glass scanner plate. My finger reached out automatically for the 'scan' button and the machinery began to spin. The temperature dropped even further.

When I turned again, Bahram had gone. Peter Lazenby was standing at the door.

'It's too late,' he said. His voice was louche, the words seemed to be dragged from him. I shook my head and pressed the 'play' button.

A voice came from the speaker. It came with such force I almost lost my balance.

'*Ma bel utta-zama ta-ni-sheti*
Mur-si-kunu-ma ekal matu . . .'

A great scream came from Lazenby's mouth. I reached for the second book and found the page and started scanning the text. The voice continued, harsh, implacable, filled with rage. Lazenby's ghost began to lose substance. His mouth opened and closed silently, still screaming. I could see the far wall through his face. I picked up a journal and flicked through it, then turned it face down and scanned another prayer. The first incantation continued. Lazenby began to shrink. I scanned a fourth text. When I looked again, Lazenby had gone. So simple, I thought.

But the house was not empty.

The first incantation ended, and the second began. A different voice this time, higher, but no less implacable. Behind it another sound: footsteps coming down the stairs from the floor above. A shadow fell across the landing. I put another text on the scanner.

A second voice joined in the incantation, then a third. The footsteps hesitated. I took up the text that was being chanted and joined in, my voice weak and halting beside those others. The spell came to an end, and I pressed 'play', and another voice lifted.

I left it playing and went out to the landing. He was on the stairs, tall, hooded, his great wings rising to the ceiling above him. A misshapen hand emerged from his sleeve, clutching his staff. The stairway was filled with flies, circling round him in homage or fear. The smell that had been in the house earlier was much stronger now. I identified it at last. It was the smell of ashes. The flies swooped and danced in the light of the lamp above my head. I thought of the Virgin Mary. I thought of her face swallowed by flies.

The voice of the chanter was joined by a woman's, then another and another, until his voice was drowned by theirs. Were Lazenby's silent victims exacting their revenge at last?

His wings rustled like dry leaves, and I thought he would lift himself up and swoop on me, but he did not. I could not see his face beneath the hood, but I felt his eyes on me. I thought of the Virgin and the flies on her blue dress.

'What is your name?' I asked.

The wings stirred. Behind us, the voices of the women were joined by those of children.

'I am all names,' he hissed.

'What name do you have here?'

'Shabbatil.'

'What other names?'

'Iblis.'

I recognized one of the words the Arabs have for him.

'What others?'

'Shaytan.'

Another Arabic name. Satan.

I reached inside my pocket and drew out the handkerchief in which I had wrapped the lump of clay from the cellar. It was still damp enough to mould. From my top pocket I took a ballpoint, and with its tip I started to incise cuneiform letters in the damp clay. His names. Shabbatil. Iblis. Shaytan. Lucifer.

The incantation stopped. He took another step towards me. The flies hummed in the silence.

I lifted the clay and slowly crushed it in my hand. Another

incantation began.

'*zi-anna zi-ki-a i-pa-de-enze-en zaazu-da khe-im-dala* . . .'

I thought of the Virgin in her black, seething gown.

He gave a cry like no cry I had ever heard before. All London heard it. He cried out, and as I watched the flies thickened and swarmed about him, growing in numbers more rapidly than I could compute. The entire stairway was filled with flies. He was covered by them, so that nothing of him could be seen.

Slowly, the flies began to disperse. The thick cloud became a curtain, the curtain a veil, and the veil nothing. When they had all gone, there was nothing left, not even the smell of ashes.

I don't know how long I stood there, speechless and motionless. A minute? An hour? How can I know?

The chanting continued a little longer, then came to a stop, and a silence like the silence after a song filled the house. I turned to go down the stairs. As I did so, the telephone rang.

I ran into the study and lifted the receiver on my desk.

'Yes?'

'Tom, it's Maeve. You've got to come right away.'

'What's wrong? Is it Nicola?'

'Don't waste any time. Just come.'

Chapter Thirty-three

Maeve was waiting for me on the doorstep.

'We've sent for a doctor,' she said. 'But the midwife doesn't hold out much hope.'

'Then the baby . . .'

She shook her head.

'Not the baby. Nicola. You'd better come up.'

They were all in the guest room—Father Shanks, the midwife, and Nicola. She looked very pale.

'I've tried to stop her losing blood,' said the midwife, 'but it's a hopeless battle.'

'Can't they give her a transfusion?'

She looked at Father Shanks.

'Maeve rang five minutes ago,' he said. 'They're getting here as quickly as they can, but . . . Your wife has injuries that are beyond help.'

The midwife looked at her, then at me.

'I think moving her will kill her. She wants to talk to you. I think you should go to her now.'

I sat down on the side of the bed. The others left the room.

'It's all over, love,' I said. 'He's gone. There's nothing to be frightened of now.'

She reached out a hand and put her fingers on my cheek.

'You're better looking than I thought,' she said.

I stared at her. She smiled—a weak but contented smile. And for the first time since I first saw her, she was smiling with her eyes.

'You can see?'

'Yes. Not very well yet, but I can see. It happened . . . during the birth. Have you seen the baby?'

'Not yet.' I had to fight to keep back the tears.

'He's in the next room. Mrs Cavendish took him in there.'

'Mrs Cavendish?'

'The midwife.' She paused. 'You look tired.'

'He's gone, love. Shabbatil, Lazenby—they're all gone.'

'Yes, you said.'

'I had to . . .'

She put her hand on my lips and shook her head.

'Let's not talk about that. I don't have much time.'

'The ambulance will be here any minute.'

'There's nothing they can do. Will you hold me?'

I took her in my arms then and held her.

'Have they found Adam yet?' she asked.

'Not yet. I'm sure they won't be long.'

'I'd like to have seen him just once.'

'You'll see him.'

She stroked my cheek, not like a blind woman now, but with the softness of a lover caressing her beloved's face.

'I always wanted to see you,' she whispered. 'And now I've seen you. I wish I could have been with you longer.' She raised herself and kissed me on the lips. And when she fell back she was heavy, and her eyes, that had been smiling before, were sightless again.

Later, when they had taken Nicola away, I sat downstairs with Maeve and Mrs Makepeace. Father Shanks was in the prayer room, clearing away the bodies of the dead flies and resanctifying everything.

'Can I see the baby?' I asked.

'Are you sure you want to?' asked Maeve.

'Not really,' I said, 'but I think I should.'

They took me upstairs to Michael's room, where a cot had been placed. I don't know what I expected to see. The baby was sleeping quietly. No horns, no tail, no claws. Just a baby, red-faced and innocent-looking.

'It's a boy,' said Maeve. 'Nicola said he was to be called after his father.'

I said nothing. I crept on tip-toe towards the cot and bent over the sleeping form. A tiny hand had crept out of the blue coverlet. He opened his eyes and looked at me. I looked at him, and I knew it was not over yet. He closed his eyes and went back to sleep. Like a baby sleeping in a world that means him no harm.

There was a phone call shortly after that to say that Seán had recovered his sight and was rapidly returning to normal. He'd have to stay under observation for a while, but his doctors were optimistic. I rang the Middlesex. Andrew and his fellow victims, save one, had all turned the corner.

When I went back to the living-room, I found Maeve and Father Shanks with the policewoman who'd been there earlier. The policewoman turned as I entered.

'Dr Alton. . . . We . . .'

'You've found the boys.'

She nodded.

'Thank God.'

'I'm afraid it's not that simple, sir.'

I looked at her, then at Maeve. Neither spoke. Father Shanks found the courage to speak up.

'Your son is all right, Dr Alton. He's down at Theobald's Road police station. It's . . . Maeve's boy has been found dead. She's just been told.'

Maeve just sat there, unable to register even this final shock. It was too much to take, on top of everything else. She'd spent the day in tears, and now that she needed grief more than ever, it was lost to her. I stumbled out a few paltry words of consolation, but my own loss was so recent, so insurmountable, all I could do was dig up clichés I'd overheard in pubs and funeral parlours reeking of stale wax.

The policewoman came up and drew me aside.

'Dr Alton, would you mind coming down to the station with me? It's about your son.'

'He's all right, isn't he?'

'Well, yes and no. I'd rather not talk here.' She looked at Maeve. 'Will you be all right with the priest here, Mrs Brennan? Or is there anyone else you'd like me to fetch?'

Maeve shook her head listlessly. Nicola would have been the one.

We left them and I fetched my coat. A police car was waiting outside. I got into the back with the policewoman while her colleague drove.

'What's happened?' I asked. 'Why is Adam in Bloomsbury?'

'He and Michael Brennan were found in the British Museum. Adam says he took some keys of yours and used them to get in without triggering an alarm. Is this possible?'

'Yes, he could have done that.'

I felt in my pocket. The keys were gone.

'They were found in a room displaying Mesopotamian material. I understand that's your field.'

'Yes.'

'They were beside a case that had been holding a new exhibit. A Babylonian god named Shabbatil. Is that familiar to you?'

I nodded.

'The case had been opened and the statue smashed with a heavy hammer. Michael Brennan was dead. His throat had been cut with a bronze knife, one of the exhibits.'

She hesitated. The spinning, emptying streets seemed to swallow us. Somewhere, far above us, there were stars, but the lights of the city blotted them out completely. It was as though nothing else existed but the streets and the grey buildings.

'Dr Alton, I don't want to say this, but I have to. We think your son killed Michael Brennan. He was holding the knife in his hand when the guard found them. Michael was lying across his lap. We haven't spoken to Adam about it yet: we don't want to do so until you're there. But we think that is what happened. Can you think of any reason why your son could have done such a thing?'

I let the silence answer for me. We drove on into the city, past the elegant and the damned, the rich and the defeated, the beautiful and the wretched. They were all his victims, either way.

Epilogue

The past is not dead, it merely sleeps. And just as you and I wait for morning, so the past waits among dreams to reawaken.

Adam is safe now, or as safe as any of us can be. He plays the flute for hours every day, and one day he may be allowed to play in public. They say he has genius. When I visit him, he plays for me.

Little Tom is five now. He's here with me in the room. We live in a small flat in Bloomsbury. He's a good child, good-looking, intelligent, companionable. I know he's waiting. I am waiting too.